Cozy Up
to Mayhem

a novel about mobsters,
witnesses, bakeries, and a cat

by Colin Conway

For the Sheep Lady

"Life is what you bake of it."

- unknown

Cozy Up
to Mayhem

Chapter 1

Sterling Carter stopped sweeping and looked up when the brass doorbell rang.

A woman in her early fifties entered Frosty Petal, the only bakery specializing in cupcakes in the small town of Wandering Springs, Washington. She immediately lowered her umbrella, shook rainwater onto the mat just inside the shop, then snapped it closed.

The customer wore a light blue jacket, blue slacks, and similar colored shoes. Her short salt and pepper hair looked recently styled. A red purse dangled over her left shoulder. She glanced toward the counter before her gaze cut to Sterling. "Afternoon."

"Afternoon," he said with a polite nod.

She looked over her shoulder and through the window. "It's coming down in buckets out there."

A storm raged outside. Occasional bursts of thunder punctuated the deluge. The weather wasn't supposed to improve for the remainder of the week.

"Holler if you find something," Sterling said before he returned to sweeping the floor.

He and the new arrival were the only two in the shop. Traffic usually slowed after the lunch hour. The bakery was busiest in the morning when folks arrived to enjoy coffee and a muffin.

Some customers came in around lunch for a cup of joe and a cupcake, but it was considerably less than the other eateries around them. Frosty Petal closed at 3 p.m. daily, not bothering to compete with the other establishments for after-work dollars. It was only a few minutes before closing time.

The woman inhaled deeply, and an appreciative smile spread across her face. "That smell."

A fresh-baked aroma filled the shop every morning, but it diminished to a fraction of its original intensity by afternoon due to repeated openings of the front door. Perhaps even time lessened the scent's impact, Sterling thought.

"How do you stand it?" the woman asked. At least one customer a day posed that question to him.

"You get used to it," he said, but that wasn't true.

Sterling didn't eat cupcakes, and he didn't enjoy muffins, either. To him, the aroma of baked goodies held as much allure as freshly poured asphalt. Now that he thought about it, he liked the smell of a recently laid blacktop better. It held the promise of adventure. Cupcakes and muffins held no excitement in his world.

The woman walked toward the glass display where rows of colorful cupcakes waited. "Where's Norma Jean?"

"At the store." Sterling swept a small pile of debris into a dustpan. "Should be back in an hour or so, but we'll be closed by then."

Overhead, a song from the 1950s played. Maybe it was the sixties. Most of the music on this radio station sounded the same to Sterling. This singer droned on about loving some girl named Peggy Sue. Sterling supposed the sentiment was fine, but he would have preferred a harder beat and at least one raging guitar solo.

"You must be new, eh?" the woman asked without looking at Sterling. Instead, her attention remained affixed on the various treats underneath the display's bright lights.

"Been here a few weeks." Sterling emptied the pan into a trash can at the end of the counter. He leaned the broom against the wall and set the dustpan on the floor. "Find anything?"

"Not much left is there?" The woman leaned left and right as she studied the remaining cupcakes. There was a single apple muffin left. "Should have gotten here earlier."

Sterling rested his hands on the top of the counter. "You from Canada?"

The woman looked up. "What gave it away?"

"Your accent," he said.

Wandering Springs resided just south of the Canadian border in Northwestern Washington. The town of Lynden was to the south. Blaine abutted the coast to the west and served as a major hub for traffic flowing in and out of Vancouver, B.C. The border crossing north of Wandering Springs was almost forgotten in comparison. Even so, in the past few weeks, Sterling had more contact with Canadians than he'd had in his entire life. It wasn't something he'd ever hoped to endure.

Thunder rumbled outside and the visitor flinched. She looked toward the street. "Haven't seen a downpour this bad in some time."

"Me either," Sterling agreed.

The customer straightened. "Guess I should introduce myself. I'm Pearl MacKenzie." She extended her hand over the counter. "Norma Jean and I have been friends for a while now."

Sterling accepted her hand and introduced himself.

Pearl eyed the still-healing scar covering the back of Sterling's hand. "Looks like that hurt."

"A little."

"Work related?"

"Something like that."

She grimaced before letting go of his hand. Pearl bent once more to study the remaining goodies. "You must be special," she said without looking up. "You're the first man Norma's ever hired."

"That so?"

"Far as I know, yeah. How'd she find you?"

"Employment agency."

Pearl's tongue appeared briefly to whet her lips. "You ever try the Neapolitan cupcakes?"

He shook his head.

"Think I'm going to give one a go." She tapped the glass above a white and brown cupcake with a dollop of pink frosting.

Sterling slipped on a plastic glove and reached into the case. "Just one?"

"Of those." Pearl looked up with a bright smile. Mischief filled her eyes. "Cupcakes are meant to be eaten in batches. That's why they're small." She winked. "'Take two, they're small,' my grandmother always said. Of course, she was talking about cookies, but I figure it goes the same for cupcakes."

Sterling opened a pink cardboard box and placed the cupcake into it.

"They never hung around long," Pearl said absently.

"The Neapolitans?"

"No, the ladies before you." She waved a hand above her head while she continued to examine the remaining cupcakes. "Seems like they all had dreams of bigger cities like Bellingham or Seattle. They dashed away with hopes of opening their own shops or meeting the men of their dreams." She tsked, then eyed Sterling. "You're not going to do that are you, Sterling Carter?"

"Look for the man of my dreams?"

She rolled her eyes. "Open your own shop."

"Not a chance."

"That's good." Her attention returned to the glass case. "Norma Jean needs someone who's stable and will hang around for a long time."

The song on the radio ended and a new one started. Now a woman sang about her boots which she proudly announced were made for walking. Sterling refrained from grunting his displeasure. What else were boots made to do? Fly? In his opinion, music before heavy metal simply wasn't very good.

Pearl looked up at him. "You like the carrot cake cupcakes?"

"I hear they're good."

She smirked. "It's a muffin with frosting. Blech." She tapped the glass. "Gimme one of those Boston Cream jobbies."

He reached into the case and grabbed a chocolate-covered cupcake with yellow cream oozing out of its center.

"Looks like that'll be a mess to eat, eh?" Pearl grinned at the apparent challenge. Her tongue darted between her lips again.

"Is that all?" Sterling asked, tucking the latest goodie into the cardboard box.

"Batches are not two." Pearl dismissively shook her head.

"You said take two because they were small."

"That's just a saying." Pearl's eyes narrowed. "Norma Jean has more to teach you, eh?"

"I suppose."

"At a minimum," Pearl said, "a batch is four." She held up as many fingers and wiggled them. "One, two, three, four."

"Got it."

Her gaze dropped to the cupcakes. "Ever eat one of these gluten-free deals?"

"Not yet."

"Don't," Pearl said with obvious disgust. "Save your stomach. It's like eating a clump of dirt." She tapped the glass again. "I'll take the last cookie dough."

Sterling removed a goodie with a top

resembling a chocolate chip cookie.

A long rumble from the storm overwhelmed the jaunty song about walking boots. Sterling didn't care for the storm, but the thunder provided welcome relief from the sixties' musical nonsense.

"You grow up around here?" Pearl asked as her gaze bounced over the remaining cupcakes.

"Just moved to town."

This surprised Pearl and she straightened, abruptly pulling her attention away from the goodies. "You moved here? To Wandering Springs?" She briefly looked out the window before returning her attention to him. "Why on earth would you do that?"

Sterling shrugged.

"Never heard of anybody doing such a thing. Seems like all the young people want to move away. Go find action elsewhere."

"Action is overrated," Sterling said.

"Tell that to the kids." Pearl bent and returned to examining the remaining treats.

Sterling had noticed a distinct lack of children in the area. The town bussed the few kids living within its boundaries to Lynden schools. At least that's what Norma Jean had told him. It seemed like a fair trade for the town of Wandering Springs—pay for gas, buses, and drivers to send the children away to school five days a week. Maybe the parents lived in Wandering Springs for that exact reason.

He believed children should be listed as a plague like they did in the bible—frogs, locusts, boils, and kids. Sterling never read the good book, but his grandmother had referenced it now and then while he was growing up. He had no idea what a locust was, but a swarm of them sounded preferable to one talkative child.

"You must like the weather or something, eh?" Pearl said.

"How's that?"

"To move here." She motioned toward the window. "Fan of the rain?"

He wasn't.

Pearl's gaze swept about the display case, and she tapped the glass once more. "I'll take the last red velvet. Leave no cupcake behind. Am I right?"

Sterling removed the treat she selected and put it in the small cardboard box. "That's four," he announced as he closed the box. "Anything else?"

Pearl looked up at him, surprised. "I guess not."

He motioned at the cash register with the box. "I'll ring you up over there."

"Of course." She slowly straightened and robotically followed him to the end of the counter. Pearl's expression darkened as she pulled a wallet from her purse. She removed her credit card and extended it to Sterling.

He quickly processed the sale. A few months prior, he worked in a mystery bookstore and bungled his way through all those transactions. He'd got quite a bit of experience working in retail sales since then. Now, the procedure was a breeze. Sterling returned the card to Pearl and smiled. "Thank you."

Pearl's expression pickled as she slipped her wallet into the purse.

"It was nice meeting you," he said. It was something he learned to utter while working in one of the other jobs. He didn't mean what he said, but it seemed people liked hearing it.

However, Pearl only frowned as she picked up the box of treats.

"I'll tell Norma Jean you said hello," he said.

She saluted him with the pink carton. "Let her know how many I bought, eh?"

"Will do." He forced his smile wider and trotted out the other phrase he'd learned from working retail. "Have a nice day."

Pearl's eyes narrowed. "You're a little thick, aren't you?"

Chapter 2

Metallica's "Motorbreath" blared through the small boombox sitting on the edge of the steel mixing table. The radio's tinny speakers didn't do justice to the heavy music, but it was better than silence. It was also better than listening to another round of tunes promoting love, peace, and harmony.

Sterling scrubbed a pan while banging his head to the third song on Metallica's debut album. He found both the small stereo and the band's cassette at a thrift store in Lynden. He picked them up for a few bucks and considered himself lucky. Every task, no matter how mundane, was always made better by his favorite music—hard, blistering metal.

He washed the pan and dropped it in a drying rack.

The music briefly paused before the opening riff of "Jump in the Fire" caused him to sharply snap his head downward. He smiled and a Zen-like calm fell over Sterling amid the blaring guitars, pounding drums, and raspy singing.

Sterling shoved his hands into the scalding water and removed a large mixing bowl. He dragged a sponge around the steel pot and realized he hadn't felt this good in a long time. This moment, with his hands in dirty, soapy water, was almost perfect.

The music clicked off and an abrupt silence filled the room. "The heck you listening to?"

He glanced over his shoulder. "Metallica."

"Sounds like a never-ending car crash," Norma Jean Bexley said. "You'll bruise my flour with all that noise."

She was a petite woman in her early seventies and more than a foot shorter than Sterling. A flour-crusted Seattle Mariners baseball cap covered her short, gray hair. Sterling had never seen her without it. She wore a quilted brown jacket, faded blue jeans, and green rubber shoes.

Norma Jean set a grocery sack on the mixing table. "How'd the rest of the day go, Silver?"

She insisted everyone, including Sterling, call her by her full name, but she loved the nickname she created for him. Sterling tried to stop her from using it early in their relationship, but she ignored his request.

"Rest of the day was fine," he said. Sterling turned his attention back to cleaning the bowl. "Pearl said hello."

"Canadian Pearl?" she asked.

He wondered how many Pearls lived in Wandering Springs. "That's the one."

"Oh, boy," Norma Jean said. She clapped twice. "How many did she buy?"

Sterling set the bowl in the drying rack. "Four."

"What?"

"I know," Sterling said, unable to hide the pride sneaking into his voice. Maybe he was better at retail sales than he gave himself credit for. "Pearl wanted to make sure I told you how many she picked up."

"I'll bet." Norma Jean clucked as she moved into his peripheral vision. "You didn't encourage her to buy more?"

"Than four? That's a batch. She said so." Sterling held up a wet hand and wiggled four fingers. He felt slightly defensive after Norma Jean's question, which was a funny feeling to develop over his skills as a salesman.

"Four's where we start," Norma Jean said. "It hardly takes any encouragement to get her to six. It's part of the game, Silver, so Pearl doesn't feel guilty." Her lips mashed together, and she grunted. "I once encouraged her up to a full dozen. Even threw in a free Rainbow Swirl to make it feel special. You know what she did?"

He eyed her.

"She sent me a thank you card. You believe that?"

Sterling recalled Pearl's expression when he closed the box after four. The pride he felt a moment ago fully evaporated.

"We need to work on your upselling, Silver." Norma Jean cocked her head. "You know what that is, don't you?"

He'd heard about upselling while working at a convenience store in Wyoming. It wasn't a skill he thought he wanted to develop.

"Still," Norma Jean said, "closing out the day with a sale of four is better than none, I suppose."

"That's what I thought." Sterling shrugged, unable to escape the disappointment he felt for not selling more cupcakes to Pearl.

Norma Jean shoved open one of the aluminum swinging doors to peer into the lobby. "How many were left when you locked the doors?"

"Nineteen."

"Bah." She let the door swing closed. It flapped several times before settling in its resting place. "That's two weeks straight with more than ten."

Sterling dried his hands with a towel. "Why don't you make less in the morning?"

"Why don't you mind your beeswax?" Her eyes immediately softened. "I'm sorry. I shouldn't bark at you."

He stared at her, emotionless. He'd been barked at by far scarier individuals than Norma Jean Bexley. A few, anyway.

"I had it down to a science," she said. "Weeks went by with no cupcakes left by closing time." Her head bobbled. "There was always a muffin or two, but muffins are like pickles."

Sterling furrowed his brow.

"They don't go with everything," Norma Jean clarified. "Cupcakes on the other hand are the perfect addition to every occasion. Good day? Celebrate with a cupcake. Bad day? Commiserate with a cupcake. Bored? Spice up your life with a cupcake. See what I mean?"

"Sure," he said.

"It's that stupid French joint." Norma Jean

flicked her hand dismissively.

Chateau Sweets was down the street. Sterling had seen it during many of his walks through the city's small downtown.

"When it opened last month," Norma Jean continued, "it ruined everything."

"You had a monopoly, you're saying."

"Darn right, I did. Now I'm competing against tarts, eclairs, and cream puffs."

Sterling didn't know what any of those words meant. Since he didn't care for sweets, he probably never would, either.

Norma Jean blew a raspberry. "I'd have baked some of that fancy junk if I thought it would've sold."

"Why not make them now? Nobody's saying you can't."

She rolled her eyes. "Listen, you stick to what you do, and I'll stick to what I do."

He raised his hands in surrender. "Whatever you say."

Norma Jean waved for him to follow. "Come on, you need to unload the groceries. Grab a coat."

Sterling dried his hands on a towel, slipped on his jacket and zipped it closed.

She eyed him with disapproval. "You need a coat with a hood."

"Too late for that. Besides, rain won't hurt me."

"You say that now. You haven't been stuck in a cold downpour with no head covering."

Sterling followed her through the shop's rear

door into a small parking lot. The only vehicle there was a small Chevrolet Bolt. Norma Jean popped open the hatchback. The rear seats were laid forward.

Fifty-pound sacks of flour and sugar were stacked on top of each other. Eight jugs of milk sat clustered together. Two boxes of supplies were pushed up against the front seats. They were filled with items like salt, vanilla extract, baking powder, and sprinkles.

Carrying heavy items was one of the requirements of Sterling's job. He lifted several bags of flour, then headed back into the kitchen.

A boom of thunder bid them farewell.

"Marion Bardot," Norma said from behind Sterling. "She's behind all my troubles."

"Who?" he asked as he gently set the bags onto the steel counter.

"The owner of Chateau Sweets. She's my rival from way back."

"Your rival how?" Sterling headed outside once more.

Norma tagged along. "We used to be friends in high school until she stole my boyfriend."

The rain pelted Sterling as he walked toward the Chevy Bolt. "You two have been around here a while."

"That an age crack?"

"Wasn't meant to be." Sterling hefted a couple bags of sugar, then headed toward the bakery. He hunched his shoulders against the rain.

Norma shuffled after him. "It wouldn't have been so bad if Cedric had turned out to be a real louse."

"Cedric the boyfriend?" Sterling set the sugar on the counter.

"Ended up her husband. Became a county commissioner, volunteer fireman, and all-around good guy." Norma angrily clapped her hands. "What a louse."

"Sounds like it."

"Don't get wise."

He smiled. "I'm assuming Cedric helped her open the French bakery."

"No, he died."

"Oh."

"It's all right," Norma said as they went outside into the rain again. "I stopped caring about Cedric years ago."

"After high school?"

"After he married what's-her-face."

"Marion," Sterling said.

She pointed into the little car. "Pick up the groceries."

Sterling asked, "When did Cedric die?"

"Couple years back." Norma's lips twisted. "Gotta say, I think ol' Cedric kept Marion distracted during their marriage and out of my hair."

"How so?"

"He was involved in a lot of stuff, so she didn't have time for any of that Frenchie nonsense. After Cedric passed, Marion had nothing but time to focus on getting back at me."

Sterling grabbed a couple bags of baking powder and straightened. "Why would she get back at you?"

"Because I was always prettier than her."

He cocked his head.

"Don't let this fool you." She waved her hand up and down her length. "I used to be a real prize."

Sterling headed into the kitchen.

"Marion couldn't do much about it after she married Cedric, especially since I got to remain footloose and fancy free."

"In Wandering Springs?"

Norma Jean's expression tightened. "You're cruising for a bruising, Silver."

He chuckled. "Just saying, this town doesn't seem like a happening place for a footloose and fancy-free gal."

She absently waved her hand. "I'll have you know I bounced around for a few years. Bellingham, Bothel, Bremerton."

"Lots of Bs."

She shrugged. "That's how it worked out."

"Eventually, you came home."

"Guess I got nostalgic."

Sterling turned on his heel and headed back to the Chevy. Norma followed along. Thunder rolled off in the distance.

Norma Jean looked into the sky and raindrops landed on her face. "Wonder if we're going to get any lightning."

"I don't mean to offend," he said, letting his thought trail off with a questioning glance.

Her gaze dropped to him. "Sounds like you're going to."

Sterling picked up four jugs of milk—two in each hand. "What's there to be nostalgic about in this town?"

"I don't know," Norma Jean said, slamming the hatch closed. "I guess I missed the people, the place, and the pace."

"Lots of Ps now."

"Pretty soon we'll make it through the whole alphabet." Norma Jean winked.

He smiled, then trudged back into the building, lowering his head against the rain. His hair felt completely wet after just a few trips.

"You're a heck of a pack mule," Norma Jean said.

"It's easy work." Sterling set the milk jugs on the steel mixing table.

"Glad to have you around on a cruddy day like today."

"I appreciate the job."

Norma Jean twisted her lips. "You know what the worst part is?"

"About the job?"

She eyed him. "About Chateau Sweets."

"What's the worst part?"

"Marion isn't even French."

Sterling unzipped his wet jacket and hung it on a nearby hook. "Bardot isn't French?"

Norma Jean scoffed. "The name might be, but Marion was born and raised here. She's as French as I am."

"But her parents—"

"Were the Van Der Hagens. That's Dutch or something." Norma Jean began sorting the groceries. "Cedric's family was the Bardots."

"This troubles you why?"

Norma Jean's eyes widened. "She opened a French bakery. Catch up, Silver. The woman is a fraud."

Sterling ran his fingers through his wet hair. "Marion opened a fake French bakery to get back at you?"

"That's what I'm saying, yes." Norma Jean clunked a bottle of honey onto the counter. "Exactly that."

"Because you were prettier."

Norma Jean put her hands on her hips. "What is it you're getting after?"

"Well, if she ended up with Cedric the good guy—"

"The louse," Norma Jean corrected, and her nose crinkled. "Good guys can be louses, too. There's no law against it."

Sterling leaned a hip against the counter. "If Marion had all those years with Cedric—"

"Must've been horrible." Norma Jean crossed her arms. "All those years of playing happy homemaker. Who'd want that? Not me, I'll tell you what." She blew another raspberry.

He waited patiently.

Norma Jean's expression tightened. "What?"

"What does Marion get out of competing with you now?"

"You don't get it."

"I'm trying to."

Norma Jean clucked. "You really are a little thick, aren't you?"

Chapter 3

"You're a little thick," U.S Marshal Lester Krumland said. "Aren't you, Beau?"

Beauregard Smith gritted his teeth and didn't respond. Krumland had been scolding him for the last several minutes.

They stood in the small parking lot of an IGA grocery store in Pacolet, South Carolina, just off State Route 9. Several black Suburbans were parked in a row. It looked like a Chevrolet dealer's lot. The nearest SUV was Krumland's. The others belonged to the marshals who recently whisked Beau out of Marlowe Bay, Georgia.

The last day was spent driving to this destination. It seemed a short distance, but there were multiple times the caravan switched directions to ensure no one was following them.

Traffic zipped by on the highway as shoppers entered and exited the grocery store. Several customers glanced at Krumland and Beau. They probably wondered what scene was occurring in their town. None had the courage to ask or even watch for too long.

Krumland rested his hand on the hood of his SUV. His upper lip curled as he studied the man under his care. "Is today the day?"

"For?"

"We send you back to jail." The marshal's

eyes darkened.

"You threatened it the last time we met."

"I should follow through with it then."

Lester Krumland was a big man. He stood eye to eye with Beau but weighed many pounds more. He wore a beige suit appropriate for the manager of a regional hotel. His printed tie contained elephants and hung too short; its tail marooned upon his belly.

Krumland was Beau's witness inspector, the latest marshal tasked with warranting his safety. Beau had turned on the Satan's Dawgs, a motorcycle club based out of Phoenix, Arizona. The prosecuting attorney called the Dawgs a criminal biker gang, but Beau had once considered them his brothers.

An FBI agent found the single weakness Beau had in his life—his love for his grandmother—and leveraged it. Beau used the money he earned through the club's illegal activities to fix his grandmother's home and later pay it off. The FBI threatened to charge her with a host of criminal accessory charges if he didn't turn rat. It was never a choice.

Fortunately for Beau, the Dawgs had lost their way since he joined them many years prior. The club's attention stopped being on each other and became focused on earning money. Beau acted as the bookkeeper, a coded reference to acting as the club's enforcer. His job was to "keep book" on those who crossed the club and clear the accounts when the time was right. Beau was good at his duties. So good, in fact, the Dawgs started lending out his skills to other clubs in exchange for money.

Sunlight glinted off the small American flag pinned to Krumland's lapel. When the marshal shifted his stance, Beau noticed the pin was upside down—a signal for an ongoing crisis. The Satan's Dawgs flew the Stars and Stripes that way inside their clubhouse and one of his brothers, a former soldier, had explained the significance to Beau.

"Looking at this?" Krumland tapped the upside-down pin. "My career is in shambles because of you."

"It's not like my life is going so great right now."

"Do tell." Krumland raised an eyebrow. "I'm all ears."

The look in the marshal's eyes told Beau it was a lie. Krumland didn't want to hear anything Beau had to say.

"Well?" the lawman asked.

"Doesn't matter."

"That's right. It doesn't matter. How many identities are we up to now?" Before Beau could answer, the marshal said, "Eight. How is that even possible?"

"There was a murder," Beau said.

"There's always a murder." The marshal smacked the Suburban's hood. "You know how that sounds?"

"Well, technically, there's not always a murder."

Krumland stared at him, dumbfounded.

"There was a robbery once," Beau said, "and the hostage situation."

"I wasn't asking for clarification."

Beau frowned.

"You're a trouble magnet." The marshal pushed off the SUV's hood and shuffled back. He hurriedly looked left and right, like an offensive lineman preparing for a blitzing linebacker. "Maybe I shouldn't stand so close to you."

"Funny."

"No, it isn't." Krumland's eyes narrowed. "Why'd you even get involved back in Marlowe Bay?"

"The cops thought I might've murdered my friend."

"You didn't, though."

"I didn't want them to smear my name."

The marshal scoffed. "It wasn't your name, Beau. The computer pulled it from the air." Krumland mimed snatching an item from the ether. "Like that."

Beau didn't think computers pulled anything from the air. "Still," he said, "I didn't want to be accused of murder."

Krumland waved a hand. "You could have disappeared and left it all behind."

"The cops wouldn't let me walk away."

"You got away from them long enough to play amateur sleuth. Right?"

Beau shrugged.

"That's enough time to find somewhere safe to call us."

"Speaking of."

Krumland's expression darkened. "What now?"

"The hotline is computerized?"

"Not anymore." Krumland sneered. "Thanks to you."

"What pencil-neck thought that was a good idea?"

"It was my idea." Krumland's jaw tightened in anger. "*Mine.*"

Beau didn't know how to take back what he just said, so he offered, "No kidding?"

"No kidding," the marshal said mockingly. He smoothed his tie then tried to pull the tail beyond his belly. It snapped back into place when he let go. "A computerized operator was something I proposed years ago to save the agency millions. The emergency dispatchers are underworked and overpaid, just waiting for someone to call in. Almost no one ever uses the call-in number."

"I have," Beau said.

"Eight times." The lawman looked at his fingers before he held up the right amount. "I'm keeping score."

"You're a witness inspector, not some analyst. Why'd they listen to you?"

"Efficiency contest," Krumland said with a gleam in his eyes. "The service asked its agents for ideas on how to improve its operations. Winners got special recognition from the Attorney General."

"What kind of recognition?"

"A certificate of appreciation."

"A piece of paper?"

"It's more than that."

"Is it?"

The marshal tsked. "We're a government agency, Beau. It's not like we can hand out bonuses whenever we want. The Attorney General answers to Congress and the accountants, after all."

Maybe Krumland's career was in worse shape than Beau thought. The idea that a certificate of appreciation served as motivation boggled his mind. It was bureaucratic thinking at its worst.

"Doesn't matter now," Krumland said. "They rolled out the computerized operator and you just had to expose its flaws. Thank you very much."

"It wasn't on purpose."

"Sort of feels that way." Krumland nodded. "I'm gonna name you Beauregard, the Destroyer of Careers."

"That's not nice."

"Are you for real? I've read your file, remember? I know everything about you."

That stung, but the marshal wasn't far off the mark. Beau was trying to be a better man since the FBI hauled him in. However, there was no escaping his history of poor decisions and bad acts. Beau hoped he'd shown himself redeemable in the months since joining the Witness Protection Program. Sadly, Krumland didn't seem to see Beau in that way.

The lawman motioned toward the east. "We've

got a marshal back in Marlowe Bay still trying to assess the damage you caused. I can't believe what I'm learning. Care to enlighten me?"

Beau didn't answer. Krumland was about to tell him all the unfortunate events that occurred during his last placement. There were plenty. Beau hoped to keep some of them secret.

"Did you know your face is on a Jacksonville news program?" the marshal asked.

"Channel 4."

Krumland's lip curled. "Why are you on the news, Beau?"

"They were covering the mystery conference when the murder happened."

"When the murder happened," the marshal parroted. "Anything ever happens to you, I'm putting that on your tombstone. Guess what?"

Beau didn't want to guess.

"The story was picked up by the national news."

"Of course it was," Beau said.

Krumland pulled his cell phone from his jacket pocket. "The marshal in Marlowe Bay texted me this. Care to explain?"

The lawman turned the device to reveal a cover for a romantic book titled *The Clues of Temptation* by author Vivienne Hart. She had been the featured speaker at the mystery conference and the book cover was prominently displayed in one of the rooms.

Underneath the blocky title was a muscular man with long flowing hair who embraced a red-haired woman. A European village burned in the background. The man bore an uncanny resemblance to Beau. It wasn't him, of course, but it sure as heck looked like him.

Beau sighed. "I can't explain it."

"Well, I can," Krumland said, turning the phone to examine the picture once more. "AI. Artificial intelligence."

"I don't understand."

"Which part?" The lawman smirked. "The artificial or the intelligence?"

Beau stared at him.

Krumland rolled his eyes. "AI is the future, Beau, and the future is now."

As far as Beau was concerned, computers were overrated. Nothing good ever came from them.

The marshal continued. "Digital artists tell the computer what they want." Krumland acted as if he was typing on a keyboard with one hand. "Then the internet spits out an image."

"My image."

"Exactly."

"How'd it get my picture?"

"Boy, you really are thick," Krumland said. "How many times have you been on social media? Do you know how many pictures of you are on the various platforms?"

Beau knew there were quite a few.

When he was in the motorcycle club, Beau lived in the shadows. The only time his picture was taken was when he was booked by the police. A Dawg's life didn't hold up well under the scrutiny of a spotlight. Since entering the

Witness Protection Program, Beau seemed as if he couldn't escape the public's eye or its fascination with social media.

"This is a serious problem," Krumland said. He showed the book cover to Beau once more. "You need surgery."

"Excuse me?"

"We need to change how you look."

"I like how I look."

"So do a million romance readers." Krumland motioned at the phone. "That book is on the bestseller list, Beau."

"Because its author was arrested."

"The lady was a bestseller before that. One of the tops according to our people."

Beau waved his hand. "No one will remember that cover in six months."

"We need to change your face." The marshal dipped his chin as his gaze dropped to Beau's hand.

"No."

"We should also get that tattoo removed."

The inky ball of fire on the back of his hand had gotten him in trouble with the law more than once. "Fine," Beau said, "take the tattoo but leave my face."

"Not sure why you're so fond of it."

"The face or the tattoo?"

Krumland crinkled his nose. "Take your pick."

"This face is mine," Beau said. "I don't have much else left."

"Whatever." The marshal slipped his phone

back into his pocket. "If we're not fixing your face—"

"My face doesn't need fixing," Beau interrupted.

"Then I need to put you somewhere no one ever wants to go."

"Minnesota?"

Krumland shook his head. "As long as I'm your inspector, you'll never go there. My home state is God's country, and I won't dishonor it with your presence."

Beau couldn't contain his smile. He had a reason to like the marshal now. Minnesota was the worst place he could imagine living besides Canada. Supposedly, everyone was overly nice, which seemed unnatural considering how cold both places were. Now that Beau considered it, Krumland wasn't especially nice. Perhaps he lost his pleasantness after leaving the Gopher State for a career in the marshal service.

"We've got one other point to discuss," the lawman said.

"What's that?"

"The woman."

Beau steeled himself. He met Daphne Winterbourne during his first placement in Pleasant Valley, and she'd been on his mind ever since. She was one of the biggest reasons for his desire to be a better man. They could never be together because Daphne would be in constant danger. Beau realized that after a member of the Satan's Dawgs kidnapped her.

Daphne recently showed up at the mystery

conference in Marlowe Bay with—

"Carrie Fenton," Krumland said. "What's up with you and her?"

"Nothing." Beau raised his hand as if appearing before a judge. "I swear."

Author Carrie Fenton had also been in Pleasant Valley. She was the first person to learn Beau was hiding in the witness protection program. She got entangled with a crazy scheme to rob a mobster and Beau rescued her.

Carrie's grandmother lived in the Chicago retirement community where Beau later worked. A murder investigation snared the visiting Carrie as a possible suspect. Once again, Beau came to her aid and helped clear her name.

Regrettably, Carrie and Daphne were witnesses to the events in Marlowe Bay. He didn't have to save either woman from bad guys or false allegations, but he got to see Daphne for a moment before he was rushed away by the marshals. Even though the assignment was a disaster, Beau considered it a success. He got to see Daphne once more.

"We're suspicious of the Fenton woman's motives," Krumland said.

"We?"

"The service." He folded his arms. "You don't know this, but Carrie Fenton is a true-crime author."

Beau did know that.

"We believe she contacted one of our witnesses about writing a book."

He knew that, too. Beau kept his expression as flat as possible. Besides himself, he knew Carrie met with two other witnesses in hiding. Alice Walker and—

"Raymond Zambotti," Krumland said, "a mob analyst. Before you interrupt, the mob is smarter than you give them credit for."

Beau believed the mob to be very smart. More so than the Satan's Dawgs.

"Unluckily for Zambotti," Krumland continued, "the mob found him before he could tell his story to Fenton."

Carrie had told Beau about her meeting with Zambotti. It sounded as if they had been careful with their conversations so neither the mob nor the marshals would find out.

"This was troubling for the service," Krumland said, "because no participant who followed the program guidelines has ever been harmed or killed. WitSec started in 1970, Beau. We're proud of that record."

"So?"

"To safeguard our record of protection, the service conducted an internal audit of Zambotti and his handler."

"Sounds official."

"You wouldn't believe. Know what the auditors found?" Krumland looked toward the street. "Zambotti wrote a phone number on the inside of one of her books. They found it when they processed his apartment after his death. That's how detailed they were. They flipped through every page in every book the man had.

Let me tell you, he had a few. That's when the auditors linked the number to Fenton."

Raymond Zambotti told Carrie Fenton about the mob's website for tracking informants hiding in the Witness Protection Program— thefbiisabunchofdirtyrats.com. It recorded sightings and showed pictures of the protected witnesses. There were even pictures rendering what the informants might look like with different hair styles and facial hair. Carrie shared that information with Beau. It was unsettling to see his name underneath the banner of "Rat." Even worse to see himself with a bald head and thick glasses.

Krumland shoved his hands into his pockets. "Imagine their surprise when the auditors learned she lives in Dover, Maine. Right around the corner from Pleasant Valley. Alice Walker's last assignment and your first."

"You think I want to write a book?"

The marshal chuckled. "I hope not. Who'd want to read about you?" He shook his head until the smile faded from his lips. "The auditors believe Carrie might suspect you're in the program. You've had contact with her in three states in a matter of months."

"Trust me," Beau said, "it's all coincidence."

"Let's hope so, because if we found a connection between you two, there's a good chance the mob will, too. If that happens..." The marshal let his thought trail off.

Beau didn't want to entertain the idea. If the mob or the Satan's Dawgs thought there was an association between him and Carrie Fenton, they'd grab her and try to exploit it somehow. It might also lead them to Daphne.

"Why are you telling me this?" Beau asked.

Krumland glanced at the other marshals. "My job is on the line. You screw up, I'm gone. You contact Carrie Fenton—"

"I won't."

"—I'm gone. She calls you—"

"I don't even have a phone now."

"—I'm gone." Krumland leaned forward. "Trust me when I say this. If I'm gone, you're gone, too. We've invested too much money and heartburn on you. The brass has had about enough."

"Back to jail," Beau said, "but I've followed the terms of my agreement."

"Besides providing information, you were to stay out of trouble."

"I have."

"Trouble is a tricky word, Beau." Krumland waggled his hands. "Lots of legal interpretations."

Beau inhaled deeply. "I want a nice quiet life. That's all."

"For you and your cat."

"That's right."

"If that's true, Beau, I'm about to give you your wish. I'm going to give you the quietest life imaginable."

"Where are you sending me?"

"Wandering Springs."

Beau's lip curled. "Sounds like a funeral

home."

"Just about. It's in Washington."

"D.C.?" Beau asked hopefully.

"Get real. It's near the Canadian border."

Beau's shoulders slumped. "You're kidding."

Krumland shook his head. "Nothing happens there—ever. You're gonna love it."

Chapter 4

Wandering Springs was like a lot of rural cities in America. Small, relaxed, and on the edge of desolation. Sterling had ridden through quite a few places like this while with the Satan's Dawgs. The townsfolk in each of those communities looked at the club with a mixture of fear and hatred.

Sterling was under no illusion now—the Dawgs were seen as a scourge when entering the town. Nothing good ever followed their arrival. Fights and thefts were commonplace during their stays, no matter how limited. Whenever the club moved on to the next town, the residents must have breathed a sigh of relief.

It had been months since Sterling felt that animosity. During his first Witness Protection assignment, he realized people looked at him differently. He no longer wore the club's cut, the leather vest with the horned dog emblazoned on its back, which was a signal for trouble as much as it was brotherhood. His long hair and thick beard were also gone now.

There was a break in the downpour when Sterling walked through downtown. Frosty Petal was at the eastern edge of the Wandering Springs Business District before it faded into residential neighborhoods. In a conventional sense, it wasn't much of a city center. Wandering Springs had a single main thoroughfare with a smattering of one-story retail and office buildings. The storefronts, however, were eclectic and well-maintained, much like Frosty Petal.

A mural of a teapot and a white cat was painted on the exterior brick walls of Peachy Keen Kitchen while Sweetheart Bistro resembled an old windmill. The buildings might have been a strange sight in a larger city, but they worked in a small town. Wandering Springs had an inordinate number of restaurants when compared to its population. Certainly, the proximity of the Canadian border kept many of these businesses profitable.

Services such as auto repairs, appliance maintenance, and banks were nonexistent in Wandering Springs. The townsfolk needed to go south to Lynden to find help in those areas or drive further west to the bustling town of Blaine.

Cozy Corner Bookshop sat a few doors away from Frosty Petal. The business name was a misnomer since the store sat midblock and didn't feel cozy inside. Someone had painted the façade to resemble a bookshelf. Three titles were shown—*The Great Catsby, Meowder on the Orient Express*, and *Purrfect Expectations*.

A bell tinkled when Sterling entered the bookstore.

Rows of towering bookshelves filled the small shop, leaving cramped walkways for customers. The tight confines made browsing titles difficult, especially for a man Sterling's size. To view the books on the lowest shelves, he squatted and leaned, often banging into the bookcase behind him.

He tolerated the narrow pathways since Cozy Corner was the only bookstore in town.

"Back for another?" Eleanor Spradlin asked.

Sterling nodded but didn't look up at the shop owner. "Need a new one for tonight."

"Fast reader," she said.

He wasn't. Sterling didn't have a television, a radio, or friends to take up his time. The only other option was knitting, a hobby taught to him by his grandmother. However, he never finished a project. Instead, he pulled the yarn free after knitting a few rows. Reading crime fiction had become his favorite pastime since his first placement in the program.

Eleanor was in her early seventies with short silver hair and a round face. She wore faded blue jeans, red Converse shoes, and a black sweatshirt with a red logo that announced CWU Wildcats.

"What're you looking for this time?" she asked.

He'd already purchased three used paperbacks since his arrival and finished them all. "Got more McGees?" he asked.

"None have come in, but I'm keeping my eyes open." Eleanor scooted closer to him. Due to the narrowness of the aisle, she couldn't pass Sterling. Eleanor pointed at a row of dusty paperbacks. "Look there. MacDonald wrote some excellent one-offs. Maybe you'd like to try one."

Sterling might but he wasn't eager. He only discovered reading a few months ago. Part of that joy was following characters like John D. MacDonald's Travis McGee and Richard Stark's Parker. He also bought the only Parker novel Eleanor had a few days ago.

Sterling glanced back at her. "What about V.I. Warshawski or *The Hot Rock* guy?"

"Dortmunder?"

"That's the one."

While at other placements, Sterling had read one novel each about V.I. Warshawski and Dortmunder. He'd happily read another.

"I'm pretty sure I'm out of both of those," Eleanor said. "They're popular with the crowd around here."

Sterling straightened and let his gaze dance over the array of colorful book spines.

"Mind if I ask you something?" Eleanor said.

"Feel free."

She hurried to the front and returned with a thick paperback. Eleanor held it up as if examining the cover while checking out Sterling's face. She flipped it around to show him. "Seen this?"

It was *The Clues of Temptation*, Vivienne Hart's latest novel. On the cover, a computer-generated muscleman stood in front of a burning village and looked eerily like Sterling. Thankfully, the redhead didn't resemble anyone he knew.

"I've seen it," he said.

"Is it you?"

"Not even close."

Eleanor flipped the book over. Her brow furrowed. "Maybe you have a twin out there."

"Let's hope not."

"Don't want the fame?"

"Something like that."

She hefted the book a couple of times. "Seems like a lot of words for some kissy face stuff."

"Haven't read it?"

"Not my cup of tea," she said, "but it's pretty popular with her arrest and all."

"Makes sense." Sterling's attention returned to browsing the titles stacked on the shelves.

"You'd have thought a mystery romance writer would've known how to get away with murder."

"Don't know anything about it," he lied.

Eleanor shrugged. "Why read her stuff now? We know she hasn't thought this stuff out. If she got away with the murder, then we'd know she was an expert."

"If she got away with it," Sterling said, "how would we know she was involved?"

"Good point." Eleanor bounced the book against her open palm. "You know, I've never asked how you're fitting in to Wandering Springs? Can't imagine it's easy since most of us have grown up together. New folks around here are as common as a four-leaf clover in a haystack."

"It's not so bad," Sterling said. "Everyone

seems nice enough."

"Any friends?"

"Can I count you?"

Eleanor smiled. "Of course."

"Then I've got two. You and Norma Jean." His gaze swept back to the books.

"What about a girlfriend?"

"I'm good," Sterling said. "Thanks."

"An attractive man like you needs to find a lady friend."

Sterling already had someone he thought about constantly. They couldn't be together because of the danger it presented her. He had no interest in meeting another woman for romance.

Eleanor tapped Sterling's shoulder with the paperback. "Maybe you could join one of those young persons' groups down in Lynden."

Sterling shook his head. Outside of the Satan's Dawgs, he had never joined anything willingly.

"Chandler," he said, snapping his fingers.

"What's that?"

He straightened and faced Eleanor. "I met someone recently who recommended a writer named Chandler. Ever hear of him?"

"You're kidding."

Sterling stared at her.

"He's probably the most famous mystery writer ever."

"I never heard of him."

"Where have you been living? Under a rock?" Eleanor shuffled down the aisle. Her eyes went toward an upper shelf and her finger tracked along the spines of various novels. "Which one do you want? *The Big Sleep. The Little Sister. The Long Goodbye.*"

"*Not Little Sister,*" Sterling said automatically.

"*The Little Sister,*" Eleanor corrected, her response just as automatic. "And why not that one?"

Sterling's mind drifted back to one particular marshal who'd insisted on calling him by that term. While Marshal Gayle Goodspeed ended up having a few good qualities, her choice of nicknames was horrible.

Instead of answering Eleanor, he asked, "Which one do you like?"

"Oh, I don't like Chandler." She waved her hand dismissively. "Tough talking private eyes aren't my preference."

"What do you like?"

"Lawerence Block."

"Never heard of him, either."

"He's wonderful," she said. "Matt Scudder and Bernie Rhodenbarr are my favorites."

"Rhodenbarr?" he asked, his eyes widening.

"Bernie Rhodenbarr, yeah. He runs a bookstore just like this." Eleanor motioned to the shelves. "Although, he leads a secret life as a professional burglar. Guess it's hard to make rent in New York selling used books."

Back in Pleasant Valley, Sterling ran a mystery bookstore. That's where he found his cat and met Daphne Winterbourne. She called the tabby Rhodenbarr since everyone entering the establishment was allowed to name the little guy so long as it was based on a mystery novel protagonist. Sterling had been so infatuated with Daphne during that first meeting he never thought to ask where the Rhodenbarr name came from.

"Anyway," Eleanor continued, "Bernie always manages to find himself in trouble." She chuckled. "Like no matter what the guy does, things always go bad."

"I understand," Sterling said.

Eleanor rested her hand on a shelf. "It might be farfetched that a professional burglar finds so much trouble, but the series is light and funny. You kind of look past the dubious nature of it all and just enjoy it. Want to start at the beginning or would you like to read my favorite?"

"Dealer's choice," he said.

She pulled a worn paperback from the row of books and handed it to Sterling. "It's always best to start at the beginning," she said.

Sterling accepted the book and read its title— *Burglars Can't Be Choosers.*

He had this book before but hadn't read it. Another bookstore owner had given him a Christmas present of three novels. Unfortunately, he left them behind when the marshals showed up and moved him to a new location.

Had he read the other copy, he might've been able to share the knowledge with Daphne Winterbourne when they recently met. He waggled the book. "I'll take this one."

Eleanor headed for the front of the store. Sterling fell in behind her.

"Seems you're hiding," she said over her shoulder.

Sterling didn't comment but slowed his walk.

When she reached the front counter, Eleanor looked back. Her brow furrowed. "I didn't mean to offend."

He forced a polite smile. "What'd you mean?"

She motioned toward the book. "A new story every few nights. No friends except for a couple old gals." Eleanor chuckled. "I know I'm old. Norma Jean knows it, too."

"I've got a cat," Sterling said.

"Well, that changes everything, doesn't it?"

He thought it did. Sterling would like a friend, but it wasn't necessary. He'd gone long stretches in prison without friends. He had associates there—men who had his back in exchange for his having theirs. They weren't friends, though. It was simple survival. Sterling once thought his fellow Dawgs were his brothers, but that belief quickly became untrue. He wouldn't call one of those men a friend now.

With his short stays at previous placements, Sterling hadn't made any deep connections. He'd met a few people who might have become true friends, given the chance. Now, he realized they were like strangers who meet during an extended hotel stay. Seen for a few days, smiles and stories exchanged, then forgotten once check-out arrives.

Only Travis the cat remained consistent in Sterling's life—a fact he initially resisted.

Eleanor tapped a couple of buttons on the cash register and announced a price. Sterling handed her a bill.

"You should find someone to spend time with," Eleanor said, dropping the change into his hand. "Nothing interesting ever happens in Wandering Springs."

"That sounds good to me."

"You say that, but it's the main reason young people leave for bigger towns."

Sterling slipped his change in his pocket. "A quiet life is what I'm after."

"You'll find that here in spades. We're boring with a capital B." Eleanor pushed the cash register drawer closed. "I just realized, maybe you should grab another book. I'm going down to Portland for a few days to visit my daughter, so you'll be stuck if you zip through this one too fast."

"Not leaving anyone to run the shop?"

"Help's hard to find around these parts." Her face brightened. "Unless you're looking to change jobs."

Sterling would love to work in a bookstore again. He didn't appreciate the opportunity the marshals gave him in Pleasant Valley. Unfortunately, he had just started working with Norma Jean. Even though the marshals got him the job, he didn't want to leave her in the lurch. Abandoning Norma Jean so he could work a job he found more fun didn't feel like the actions of a better man.

"Maybe I can help on my days off," Sterling suggested. He didn't do anything with his free time anyway.

Eleanor smiled. "That'd be wonderful. We'll talk about it when I get back." She grabbed *The Clues of Temptation.* "Interested in reading this? I'll loan it to you, and you bring it back when you're done."

Sterling shrugged a single shoulder. "Sure. Why not?"

She handed him the book. "Better to be prepared I always say."

***

Dark clouds hung overhead, threatening to release another deluge.

Sterling continued down Main Street, eventually crossing to the other side of the road. Chateau Sweets stood at the west end of the retail strip, the furthest away from Frosty Petal without leaving downtown. Once Sterling passed the French bakery, he'd turn north into a residential neighborhood and walk a few more blocks to the small house the marshals had selected for him.

A pink and white striped awning was attached to the brown brick façade of the French bakery. A man stepped out of the establishment. A thin loaf of bread peeked out of the paper bag he held.

An older woman held the door open after the

customer left. "Thanks for stopping in," she called.

The man lifted the sack in a show of appreciation.

The woman's eyes cut to Sterling. Her shoulder-length hair looked richly brown, an unnatural shade for her age, but she wore it well. A white apron protected her blue dress. Sterling imagined the woman would have been quite striking in her youth.

"I heard about you," the woman said, a smile forming. "You're the new man in town."

Sterling stopped walking. "Guilty as charged," he said, surprised at the words that slipped through his lips. He had certainly never uttered those words in a courtroom. Judges always did that for him.

The woman stepped completely out of the bakery. She walked down the few steps toward Sterling with her hand extended. "Marion Bardot."

He accepted her hand and they shook. Sterling introduced himself.

"What brought you to Wandering Springs?" Marion asked.

"A job."

"Working with Norma Jean?" Marion raised an inquisitive eyebrow. "Are you part of her family?"

"Just a guy in need of a paycheck."

Marion crossed her arms as she studied Sterling. "You don't look the type for cupcakes."

"You know how it is."

"Actually, I don't. Why don't you tell me?"

He needed to come up with a better story. It seemed a man in his thirties choosing to move to Wandering Springs was a highly suspect decision in the minds of the locals. Sterling waved politely to end the conversation. "Have a nice day."

"Hold on," Marion said. She moved closer. "What's Norma Jean got you doing in her shop?"

It seemed a harmless enough query, especially since she abandoned the question of why he moved to Wandering Springs.

Sterling said, "She's got me cleaning mostly."

"Dishes and whatnot?"

"Some cashier duties, too."

Marion's eyes narrowed. "She teaching you how to bake those God-awful cupcakes?" Her upper lip curled.

"Not yet," Sterling said, "but she said she will."

"Don't think of that as a benefit. You can learn how from the back of a box." Marion glanced down the street. "What's she paying you?"

Sterling didn't feel comfortable telling her. Norma Jean couldn't pay a lot but that was fine. He didn't have many needs.

"You know what?" Marion waved her hand to dismiss the question. "Doesn't matter."

"All right." Sterling turned to leave. "Have a good one."

"I'll pay you more," Marion said hurriedly. She took another step closer to Sterling, standing right next to him now, and looking up with eager eyes. "How's fifty percent over what you're making with Norma Jean?"

"I'm sorry—" Sterling started, but Marion raised her hand, cutting him off.

"Seventy-five percent," she said. "That's the highest I can go."

"Thank you for the offer, but—"

Marion frowned. "Sterling, I'm in desperate need of help."

"If I work for you, then Norma Jean's in a pinch."

"We'll consider that a bonus." Marion winked.

"I'll pass," Sterling said, "but thanks for the offer."

She grabbed his arm to stop him from leaving. "Double. I'll pay you a hundred percent more than she's paying you."

Sterling gently pried her fingers from his arm. "I'm sorry."

Marion's expression darkened. "Have it your way but Norma Jean will be out of business in six weeks. Mark my words." She waggled a finger at him. "When she is, don't come to me looking for work."

"Okay," Sterling said and stepped away from her.

"Wait." Marion hurried in front of him and held up her hands for him to stop walking. "I'm kidding. I'd hire you if she went out of business. Of course, I would." Her head bobbled. "Maybe not at double. That's a one-time offer."

"Talk with you later." Sterling stepped around

her and headed for his house.

"Stop in for a croissant some time," Marion called from behind him. "We'll see if we can work a deal!"

***

Sterling lived in a two-bedroom house on Evergreen Road. The town's north-south thoroughfares were named after trees—Hemlock Road, Alder Road, etc. Except for Main Street, the east-west streets were named after fruits—Apple Road, Strawberry Road, for example. There weren't many streets in either direction so the naming convention could afford to be simple.

When he stepped into his house, Sterling heard a rumbling in another room. It sounded like a small horse. An orange cat trotted into the living room. It stopped once it entered and considered Sterling.

"Hey, buddy," Sterling said.

Travis trilled, then darted behind the couch.

Sterling had grown fond of the cat over the past few months. Lately, he had hoped the tom would bond with him, but the cat's affection for him was the same as Sterling's for children. They were better seen than heard, and they were better out of sight than seen. Sterling fed, watered, and cleaned up after Travis, but the cat had no interest in showing any real appreciation.

He might occasionally rub against Sterling's

leg, but it was a mind game. When Sterling went to pet the cat, Travis would bolt. Still, it was better than being alone.

Perhaps Eleanor Spradlin was right—maybe he needed a friend.

Sterling opened the refrigerator and considered his dinner options. He didn't have much to begin with—he lived a modest life and had a simple palate. He closed the refrigerator and moved to a cabinet containing cans of chili, beef stew, ramen packets, and granola bars.

He selected a packet of ramen, then filled a pan with water and started the stove. While he waited for the water to reach a boil, Sterling's thoughts returned to his life.

His own actions and choices brought him to Wandering Springs. He was under no illusion otherwise. Blaming the FBI agent who caught him or the marshal who chose this location removed his responsibility in the matter. That wasn't what a better man would do.

Sterling checked the cat's bowls while waiting. The little guy still had plenty of kibbles and water. Travis lay in the middle of the living room now, watching him. His tail lifted and fell rhythmically. Sterling couldn't tell if the tom was content or irritated.

He crossed his arms and rested his back against the counter. Travis stared at him, and Sterling stared back. "Two can play this game," he said. The cat seemed unimpressed by Sterling's tough guy routine.

As the Satan's Dawgs' bookkeeper, Sterling

was the toughest man in the club house. He was responsible for dealing punishment to those who crossed the Dawgs. The penance could be anything from a simple beating to something permanent.

Now that Sterling thought about it, the beatings were never simple. Everyone involved in those moments carried around the memories. Some were physical. His were mental. There had been plenty of times that Sterling felt completely justified in thumping someone. However, there were more than a few times he meted out the Dawgs' version of justice to someone undeserving of such violence.

Travis flopped to his back and looked toward the ceiling.

"I win," Sterling said.

The water on the stove came to a boil. He ripped open the small package, removed the flavor packet, and dumped the noodles in. Sterling swirled the pan's contents with a wooden spoon.

Even though he struggled with bouts of loneliness, Sterling thought his current situation was better than the one he had with the Satan's Dawgs. In Phoenix, his life felt hollow. He could never truly get close to the other guys in the club. What was worse, he could never tell his grandmother what he did.

Being a bookkeeper was a solitary existence. The other Dawgs thought the position held prestige and a certain amount of power. Sterling received wide latitude for the skills he brought to the club. The guys considered it weird he never cursed—a trait taught to him by his grandmother—but they never pressed the issue. When the other Dawgs turned to women and alcohol to blow off steam, Sterling's former self knitted.

Unfortunately, his grandmother learned about Sterling's life with the Dawgs after his FBI arrest. He couldn't contact her now because he worried the club might be watching. He didn't fear the Dawgs would grab Ma and use her as bait. There was an unwritten code among the club that mothers and grandmothers were off limits. Fathers, on the other hand, were fair game. Sterling had never met his, so he had no concerns about the man's safety.

Sterling poured in the flavor packet as he continued to stir the noodles. A spicy aroma drifted up from the boiling water.

He held the flavor packet up so the cat could see it. "Want some on your kibbles?"

Travis stopped playing with a kicker toy to briefly eye Sterling, then returned to attacking the pretend fish.

Sterling tossed the packet in the trash. He wouldn't have put any on the cat's food. He wasn't a maniac.

On nights like this, which felt like most evenings now, Sterling's thoughts eventually landed on Daphne Winterbourne. Until he saw her, Sterling had never believed in love at first sight. It was a silly and ultimately hazardous trait to consider while with the Dawgs.

Relationships were transactional, and love was something to be weaponized by either person involved.

There were always women around the Satan's Dawgs. The club's aura of danger attracted the hang-around girls. They seemed to thrive on the rough and degrading treatment the Dawgs gave them. Sterling spent time with most of the hang-around girls, but he considered none of them special, any more than they saw past the leather vest he wore.

Daphne Winterbourne quickly secured a significant place in his heart, and he was only in Pleasant Valley for a week before he fled for his safety and hers. The two had kissed twice prior to his departure. He remembered both clearly—the touch of her lips, the cant of her head, and how he felt afterward. Sterling couldn't recall a single kiss from any of the hang-around girls and there had been plenty of moments from which to choose.

Sterling turned off the stove and poured the ramen soup into a bowl. He set it on the counter, standing while he ate.

Travis hopped up, then scampered into the bedroom. The cat did that often—sprinting in and out of rooms for no apparent reason.

Sterling might have eventually grown beyond his infatuation with Daphne. His grandmother once told him time healed all wounds, and he believed it probably involved matters of the heart, too. Instead, those memories of infatuation intensified after seeing Daphne at the mystery conference last month. The event was held at a hotel where Sterling worked as a porter.

His name wasn't Sterling then. It also wasn't the name Daphne had known while he was in Maine nor was it his real name. With Daphne, it didn't seem to matter what name he had assumed. The moment they made eye contact, however brief, his heart picked up right where it left off.

Before he had to flee his last assignment, he went in for a last kiss, but Sterling's actions and choices interrupted the moment. Even though he wanted to, he couldn't blame anyone for missing the opportunity to kiss Daphne again except himself.

Sterling swirled his fork through the noodles but didn't lift any from the bowl.

Sadly, he couldn't call Daphne. He couldn't send letters or gifts. Not even an email. The Dawgs and the criminal network they were tied into might be able to trace Daphne through him. One Dawg had discovered some postcards Sterling once planned to send her. Had that man gotten the information to the club, she'd forever be in jeopardy. Sterling ensured the man would never bring harm to her.

He set his fork down without eating, then pushed the bowl away. His appetite had faded. Maybe he'd finish the noodles later.

Sterling knew what was right, and what needed to be done. That didn't make it easier, and it certainly didn't mean he had to like it. His quest to be a better man was harder than he would have expected.

Sterling grabbed the paperback he bought earlier, Lawrence Block's *Burglars Can't be Choosers*, and settled into a chair.

It was another quiet night in Wandering Springs. If all went well, it was how he'd spend the rest of his life. The idea didn't fill him with happiness.

Chapter 5

Sterling walked to Frosty Petal Bakery every morning under the cover of darkness. It was no different this morning except he hunched his shoulders and bowed his head against the once again pouring rain. The storm was expected to hang around for another day. Sterling shoved his hands into his jacket pockets to stave off the chill. He'd arrive at the bakery soon enough and get dry and warm then.

The marshal service gave him a beat-up Honda. He'd only driven it once since his arrival when he spent an afternoon in Lynden. The car didn't start this morning, likely a dead battery. Sterling didn't have the time to investigate the problem. It would give him something to do after work today.

Overhead, thunder boomed.

Maybe Sterling would wait to work on the Honda until the rain stopped.

He usually didn't mind walking to the bakery. Wandering Springs was small, and he liked being outside without the fear of the Satan's Dawgs or the mob breathing down his neck. The rain dampened his enthusiasm for the outdoors but didn't fully erase it. Wet, cold, and free was better than dry, warm, and dead any day.

Sterling hunched his shoulders a little higher and walked faster.

Wandering Springs was quiet at this hour. Most of its residents were still tucked away in their beds. Bakers and their assistants, however, did not have that luxury. As he passed Chateau Sweets, Sterling noticed a light on in the back. Marion Bardot was likely prepping the day's treats much like Norma Jean would be. He briefly thought about the two women until he was forced to navigate around a couple of large puddles in the road on his way to the far sidewalk.

City lights illuminated Main Street. Sterling's shadow moved around him as he passed through the halo of lights.

A dark sedan drove slowly down Main Street. It was odd to see a car at this time of morning. The border crossing didn't open until 8 a.m. Perhaps this was an out-of-towner who didn't know and now had to waste four hours.

The black BMW slowed as it passed Sterling. Its white front license plate read *Beautiful British Columbia* in blue letters. The driver's window was down and the man behind the steering wheel eyed Sterling with suspicion. It appeared there might be someone in the passenger seat. The back windows were tinted dark.

Sterling couldn't get a good look at the driver. The morning's darkness and the distance precluded him knowing much more than the man was white and bald. Something was off about the driver. Sterling couldn't put his finger on it, but he'd been in enough hinky situations to trust his gut. He straightened to his full height, lifted his head, and took his hands out of his pockets. If trouble was coming, he wouldn't face it bowing to the rain.

The driver continued to watch Sterling until the dark sedan slowly passed by.

Sterling fought the urge to run. Surely, the Dawgs and the mob hadn't found him in Wandering Springs. He'd been there only a few weeks, and the days had all been quiet with the same routine. Up early, go to work, go home, stay out of trouble.

Since arriving in Northwestern Washington, he strictly followed the rules laid down by his first witness inspector.

Do not contact people from your old life.

Do not visit places from your old life.

Do not develop habits from your old life.

They weren't hard to remember, and he didn't have the desire to break any of them.

The BMW drove down the street and turned at the next block.

Sterling relaxed, then shrugged off his concern. Perhaps the situation was as he first thought—an out-of-towner who didn't know what time the border opened. If the Canadian driver missed returning to the Great White North last night before the gates closed at midnight, he would have been stuck in the area for eight hours.

Sterling knew some of the crossings stayed open twenty-four hours—Norma Jean had told him so. He didn't know much about getting into

Canada. It wasn't something he ever planned to do. Sterling wanted to be a better man, but Canada's culture of niceness irritated him. No one was that kind, he believed, especially not a whole country. Either all Canada's residents faked being pleasant, or it was a marketing scheme to encourage Americans to visit and spend their money. Whichever it was, Sterling wasn't buying.

Perhaps driving to the next border crossing was too much trouble for the Canadian and his passenger. Certainly driving to Lynden and getting a hotel room wasn't that much effort. So why cruise around Wandering Springs? Maybe they were short on cash and couldn't afford a place for the night.

Sterling could what-if the situation to death. None of that mattered now since the car and its occupants were no longer a concern. He hunched his shoulders and lowered his head against the rain.

An engine revved from behind Sterling, and he glanced back. Headlights approached on his side of the road now. He straightened and lifted a hand to shield his eyes.

The urge to run coursed through his veins. Sterling hated the feeling even though he'd run plenty in his life. If something bad was about to occur, he wanted to stay and fight. However, he had no weapon and was in the open. Sometimes fleeing was the best option, if only to find a better place to fight.

The car slowed, and the headlights flicked off.

Sterling lowered his hand. A different car, a white Lexus, pulled close to the curb. Beau eyed it with suspicion. Two cars this time of morning wasn't right. The wiper blades continued to flick rain from the windshield. The passenger side window rolled down.

"Hey, you," a man said, "come here for a second."

Sterling tamped down his concerns and walked closer to the white sedan. Rain splattered against the door and into the car. The passenger didn't seem to mind. Sterling leaned slightly to see the driver. A woman behind the wheel watched him with disdain. His gaze shifted to the back seat where someone else sat, but due to the morning's darkness, Sterling couldn't clearly make the person out.

"Don't look at him," the man in the passenger seat said. "Look at me."

"What can I do for you?" Sterling asked, mustering as much politeness as he could.

The passenger wore a black jacket over a black turtleneck shirt. His manicured stubble looked like a disguise of masculinity. "You know the owner of the cupcake store?"

Sterling glanced down the street. "It doesn't open for a couple hours."

"That wasn't what I asked," the passenger said.

The woman leaned over so she could eye Sterling. She had short blond hair and a severe stare. She wore a button-up shirt underneath her suit jacket. "You look familiar, eh. Where do

I know you from?"

Sterling shrugged. "No idea."

"Cupcake store?" the passenger reminded.

"I don't know the owner," Sterling said. It seemed an appropriate time to lie.

The passenger and the driver exchanged glances.

"From around here?" the woman asked.

"Just moved to town," Sterling said.

The man in the passenger seat asked, "What're you doing out so early?"

Sterling waved absently as he searched for another lie. "My cat ran away."

Rain ran down his forehead and Sterling's hands were cold. He didn't dare put them in his pockets.

The wipers continued to flick water from the windshield of the Lexus—*thwip, thwip, thwip.*

A hand appeared from the darkness of the back seat and landed on the passenger's shoulder. "Ask him what kind of cat," a deep male voice said. The hand slipped back into the darkness.

"What kind of cat?" the passenger echoed.

"Orange." Sterling thumbed down the street. "I need to get going."

"Hold on," the driver said. She tapped the arm of the man in the passenger seat. "This guy doesn't look familiar to you?"

The man in the passenger seat considered Sterling for a moment. "Nope."

The driver leaned further across the car to study Sterling. "Ever have long hair?"

Sterling stiffened. He'd worn his hair long since high school. He only cut it after the marshals insisted upon his entering the Witness Protection Program.

"Open the box," the driver said, not taking her eyes off Sterling.

The glove compartment popped open into the passenger's hands. Inside was a gun and a paperback. The driver pulled out the book and lifted it. "I knew it."

"Lemme see," the passenger said. He grabbed the novel from the woman and flipped it over. "*The Clues of Temptation*? I can't believe you read this garbage, Lark."

"Yeah?" the driver asked, her gaze slowly turning to the passenger. "You can't believe what, Theo?" She emphasized the passenger's name and glared at him.

Theo seemed confused. "What'd I do?"

"You used my name."

"Yeah, but you said mine."

The man in the back snapped his fingers and stuck his hand over the seat. "Gimme."

"Sure thing, boss," Theo said, giving up the book.

Once again, Sterling tried to get a look into the back seat.

"Hey," Lark said. "Eyes over here, Temptation."

Theo spun in his seat. "What were you doing?"

Sterling casually leaned on the door with both hands. Rain pelted his neck and ran underneath his jacket. The cold was starting to bother him, but he did his best to ignore it. "Why are you looking for the owner of the cupcake bakery?"

"Too close," Theo said, his brow tightening. "Step back."

"Now you know her?" Lark asked.

"Something ain't right," the man in the back seat said. "Both of you get out and ask your questions more vigorously this time."

Theo rolled his eyes. "Look at what you did. Now, we gotta step out in this rain."

"You're gonna pay for ruining my hair, Temptation." Lark angrily jammed the transmission into Park. She popped open her door and reached her hand inside her jacket.

"I don't know the owner," Sterling said, letting go of the door, "but when it opens, I can tell her you're looking for her."

"When the store opens," Lark said, "we can tell her ourselves."

"If you don't know her," Theo said, "why would you let her know?" He opened the passenger door and took one foot out.

Sterling lifted his hands in mock surrender. "I don't want any trouble," he said. He didn't like playing possum with these three, but if he didn't have to tangle with them, his identity could remain intact.

The man in the back seat reached out and held Theo's shoulder. "Forget it. This one doesn't know nothing."

"You got lucky," Theo said to Sterling. He

pulled his leg back into the car and closed the door.

"So lucky," Lark added. She removed her hand from the inside of her jacket and dropped the car into Drive.

"If you see a cat..." Sterling said, letting his earlier lie hang unfinished.

Theo faced forward as the passenger's window slowly closed. He bent forward and looked up through the windshield, obviously checking out the pouring rain.

Sterling stared at himself in the reflection of the tinted glass as the white Lexus slowly pulled away. Above the numbers on the rear license plate were the words *Beautiful British Columbia.*

***

Sterling hurried down Main Street to Frosty Petal. Since the hoods in the Lexus asked about the owner of the cupcake bakery, it was likely they'd already been by the store and found no one there. Regardless, Sterling had to check to make sure.

Norma Jean always arrived before Sterling. If she was working, the kitchen lights would be on, much like they had been at Chateau Sweets.

Sterling didn't run because he worried the occupants of the Lexus or BMW might be lurking in the shadows or hiding around a nearby corner. He'd have a tough time explaining why he sprinted directly to Frosty Petal.

That's why he called out, "Travis!" as he acted like he was looking for his missing cat.

Sterling felt foolish for doing so, but he'd been forced to pretend before. While with the Satan's Dawgs, Sterling acted all the time. He often wore an emotional mask to disguise his feelings with his brothers in the club. He donned the mask while carrying out the bookkeeper's responsibilities. During contacts with law enforcement, he often pretended to be innocent, sometimes with surprising results.

His need to act hadn't stopped since joining the Witness Protection Program. It intensified. Every day, Sterling pretended he was someone different. He carried on a perpetual lie. It might sound exhausting to an outsider, but it wasn't so bad. That's why Sterling occasionally imagined himself a pretty good actor. Maybe he should have tried out for the high school play or joined the prison's drama club. Those were opportunities long gone.

"Travis!" he shouted, then added, "Hey, buddy!" to show additional concern just in case any of the goons were watching.

Sterling felt certain the occupants of the black BMW and white Lexus were tied together. That meant they were all looking for Norma Jean. What had she done to warrant their interest? It was too much to hope this was all about a bad cupcake.

If he knew Norma Jean's phone number, he could call her. He knew the shop's number, but it didn't matter, since the burner phone he bought was safely tucked underneath a pillow at his house. Sterling never carried the phone with him because he didn't want the temptation to call someone like his grandmother or Daphne Winterbourne.

No phone numbers were stored in the cheap phone. Doing so was considered a violation of operational security. It was okay because he only needed to remember a couple of numbers—the U.S. Marshal's emergency hotline and the FBI agent who first arrested him. The former changed every time he ended up with a new assignment while the latter remained the same. He didn't need to call either right now.

"Travis!" Sterling yelled as he neared Frosty Petal.

The bakery was dark this morning. Sterling didn't enter through the front door. If anyone was watching, he didn't want to dawdle at Frosty Petal's entrance. Instead, he continued to the end of the block and crossed the street, hopping over a large puddle in the process. Sterling walked into a neighborhood comprised of small homes with neatly kept yards. He bent as if to look behind a small bush. The play had to go on.

A thunderclap broke the early morning silence, and the rain seemed to intensify.

Sterling needed to find Norma Jean. Unfortunately, he didn't know where she lived. Even though Wandering Springs was a small town, Norma Jean never mentioned her home. He didn't consider that unusual as it hadn't come up as a topic of conversation.

A black BMW appeared from a side street and crept toward him. Its British Columbia license plate revealed it was the same car as earlier. The windshield wipers flicked rain away. The driver's window was up this time as it slowly passed by. However, Sterling knew the vehicle's occupants were watching him.

He cupped his hands and hollered, "Travis!"

The luxury sedan continued down Main Street and Sterling turned at Ponderosa Road. Now he had to risk doubling back to the bakery.

***

Sterling worried a car full of Canadians might roll through the alley at any moment. If that happened, he didn't need to make their job easier. He reached up and quickly unscrewed the lightbulb above the rear entrance to Frosty Petal. Complete darkness fell over the rear stoop.

The alley remained awash in shadows since a single light pole stood guard back there. However, it didn't illuminate the bakery or its small parking area.

Sterling had keys to Frosty Petal's doors, both front and back, as he was responsible for closing the shop. It took a moment of fumbling with the lock, and he was inside. Sterling secured the door behind him.

Blackness bathed the shop's interior. Norma Jean's office was near the back. Sterling ran his hand along the wall until he found the opening, and slipped in. He closed the door behind him and flicked on the light. The room was windowless, so he wasn't worried about light seeping out and betraying him to any passersby.

Sterling sat at Norma Jean's desk and hurriedly yanked open its three drawers. He searched for anything that might have her home address or phone number on it. Sterling lifted out stacks of papers and scanned each one.

The only address listed belonged to the bakery. He shoved the papers back where he found them.

The business still had a desk phone, and he pulled it closer to him. Perhaps Norma Jean had her home number saved in there in case a worker ever needed to call her. Ten blank spots sat next to as many small gray buttons. Figured, Sterling thought, what kind of emergency would a cupcake bakery have? A frosting shortage? He pushed the phone away.

A small puddle had formed under his chair, the result of rainwater dripping from Sterling's clothes and boots. A chill ran up his spine. It wasn't very warm in the bakery since Norma Jean primarily used the working ovens to heat the small building in the morning. Sterling could turn on the heater, but he didn't plan to stick around Frosty Petal long enough for it to matter.

He leaned back in the chair and crossed his arms. Sterling's gaze drifted to the posters that various state and federal agencies required an employer display. There was information about payroll deductions, worker's compensation, and reporting workplace accidents.

Sterling focused on a small card pinned to the wall. Norma Jean had tacked her state-issued food server permit next to the doorjamb. Sterling had a permit, too, but he never took a test for it. Marshal Krumland handed the small card to Sterling along with his new placement packet. Since the first day Sterling received it, the card remained tucked safely in Sterling's wallet in case the state's Health Department ever showed up to conduct a surprise inspection.

Norma Jean said the health officials usually came once a year to Wandering Springs since the town was so remote, and they scheduled visits to all the town's restaurants so as not to waste a trip. Still, Sterling thought it best to not take chances and carried the card with him. He hadn't looked at his permit since that first day and couldn't remember if an address was written on it.

He rose to his feet, hopeful. Norma Jean's name and signature were on her permit along with an expiration date only a month away. However, her address wasn't listed. Sterling grunted and flopped back into his seat. It would've been too easy.

Sterling pulled all the papers from the desk drawers and reviewed them once more. He took his time, but the result was the same—no address.

He found the bakery's checkbook, but the shop's address was listed in the upper left corner. Sterling tossed the book into the drawer.

There were options to finding her, of course.

He could try the internet if he was prone to doing such a thing. Sterling only had a little experience with computers. The Dawgs rewarded brawn over brains, so they forced the prospects and the hang-around girls to do any computer work.

Sterling imagined one of the people looking for Norma Jean would've used the internet to search for her. She didn't have a computer in the bakery's office, and she'd complained vigorously about technology in the past. Perhaps she was one of the lucky few not to have their name plastered all over the world wide web.

The morning was still young; it was barely after four. Sterling could walk through the entire town, knocking on doors until he found Norma Jean. It wouldn't take all day to do that. However, his actions would surely create a stir. Lights flicking on throughout neighborhoods would attract the attention of the occupants of either the Lexus or the BMW.

As distasteful as it was, Sterling could call the county sheriff.

Wandering Springs didn't have a police department, so they relied on the Whatcom County Sheriff's Office for law enforcement services. Norma Jean had told Sterling this during his initial days at the bakery. As such, the agency had a large area in Northeastern Washington to cover. If Sterling called for help right now, what would he say? Norma Jean was late to work, and two carloads of Canadian thugs were looking for her?

Sterling scoffed. He always considered Canadians about as dangerous as decaffeinated coffee or toothless lapdogs. Perhaps he'd been wrong in that assessment but now wasn't the time to reconsider his position on citizens of the Great White North.

Perhaps Sterling could contact a neighboring business and ask the owner or an employee if they knew where Norma Jean lived. Certainly, someone who worked on Main Street would know.

Sterling's gaze drifted to the clock on the wall. No businesses opened at this hour. It'd be some time before Main Street welcomed paying customers.

However, Sterling knew of one other person working at this time.

Chapter 6

Sterling returned to Main Street. Darkness continued to blanket Wandering Springs, and the light poles cast rings of illumination over the road and its sidewalks. All the shops on Main Street remained shuttered at this hour.

He shoved his hands in his pockets and hunched his shoulders against the rain and cold. He didn't hurry, though. Instead, he returned to the act of searching for a runaway cat.

"Travis!" he shouted.

Sterling tried to sell his concern in case any of the Canadian thugs were still watching. His head swiveled as he pretended to investigate every shadow. The act was half-hearted, and not nearly as convincing as earlier.

Rain soaked his hair and jeans. His lightweight jacket wasn't completely waterproof. It kept most of the rain from his torso but didn't stop the cold from working its way up his legs or down his neck. Sterling had a brief respite from the weather when he entered Frosty Petal. Now, back in the elements, his enthusiasm for pretending waned.

"Travis," he said.

Sterling had gotten away with plenty of bad actions during his life, whether it be petty theft while in high school or major felonies as a Dawg, because he always committed to the lie, no matter what it may have been.

When he was younger, Sterling didn't consider pretending an important part of survival. His freedom relied upon convincing nosy citizens and eager cops that he wasn't the type to steal a bottle of beer or inflict serious bodily harm on a member of a rival club. Sterling was much better at convincing citizens rather than the police.

"Travis," he muttered.

His pace had quickened, a direct correlation to the pelting rain. Sterling shivered from the cold and hunched his shoulders even higher. He shoved his hands deeper into his pockets.

A couple of blocks ahead, the white Lexus turned onto Main Street, its headlights swinging in Sterling's direction. The car immediately pulled to the curb.

Sterling slowed as he heard another car approach from behind. He glanced over his shoulder as the black BMW slowly passed. The driver's window was slightly lowered, just enough to reveal the driver glancing in Sterling's direction.

It crossed into the opposite lane of traffic, which wasn't a dangerous action at this time of morning. Then the BMW stopped when it reached the Lexus. The two cars pointed in opposite directions so the drivers could easily communicate through their open windows.

The Lexus flashed its headlights. Sterling waved at the car, then hollered, "Travis!"

Canadians in luxury automobiles, he mused. A strange thought occurred to Sterling then. He wondered if any company in the Great White North manufactured cars. He had plenty of reasons to dislike Canada but lacking their own automobile was certainly a viable reason Sterling could add to their list of unfavorable qualities. The idea made him smile since he didn't want to change his opinion about the U.S.'s northern neighbor.

Perhaps it was the weather, but the cold and rain had a negative effect on his desire to be a better man.

He crossed the road before he passed the two sedans. Sterling didn't want any of the vehicles' occupants to be encouraged to call out to him.

"Travis!" he shouted in the middle of the street.

Sterling kept walking and eventually passed Chateau Sweets. The light burned in the kitchen. He didn't climb the steps to the front door, however. Not while the Canadians could see him.

He continued to the end of the block and turned. He glanced back at the luxury sedans and discovered they were gone.

Sterling hurried toward the nearest alley and entered it. He doubled back toward Chateau Sweets. The only lights back here were from the businesses fronting Main Street and the residences lining the street to the north. The pole light directly behind the French bakery was burned out. Sterling crouched, prepared to run, but stopped himself. Sprinting through the shadows could draw attention. He righted himself and continued at a purposeful pace.

A small, asphalted lot sat behind Chateau Sweets with a red Subaru parked nearest the stairs.

Sterling sauntered to the shop's back door and softly knocked. He glanced up and down the alley, concerned the Canadians might show up at any moment.

The door pulled back slightly, and an eye appeared in the opening. "Hello?"

"It's me," Sterling said, then added his name for good measure. "From Frosty Petal."

"Why yes, it is." Marion Bardot opened the door wider. She wore a black apron over a white shirt and blue jeans. Flour covered the apron and her hands. Marion brushed away a wisp of hair from her forehead. "A little early to take me up on my job offer."

"I need your help."

"That sounds ominous." Her grin faded.

"Can I come in?"

Marion asked, "What's going on?" as she stepped back, a silent invitation for him to enter.

Sterling slipped by her and into the French bakery's kitchen. He made sure they were out of sight from the front windows. Marion closed the door behind him.

"Lock it," Sterling said.

Her expression tightened as she studied him. "You're dripping all over my floor. What're you doing out in this rain?"

"Avoiding Canadians." He thumbed over his shoulder. "Four men and a woman."

Marion furrowed her brow. "You're not making sense."

"They're looking for Norma Jean."

She crossed her arms. "What's that got to do with me?"

"She's not at the Frosty Petal."

"The cupcakery." Marion's expression soured. "I need to find her."

Marion waved toward the ovens. "And I need to get back to baking."

Sterling sighed. "What about the Canadians?"

"What about them? They're probably waiting for the border to open."

"They're mobsters," Sterling said.

"Canadian mobsters are looking for Norma Jean?"

"That's right. I think she's in real danger."

Marion cocked her head. "Then you should call the cops."

"And say what? We suspect some Canadian thugs are looking for Norma Jean?"

"*We* don't suspect anything," Marion said. "You're the one with this cockamamie idea about Canadian mobsters in Wandering Springs." She moved to an oven and peered in. "I don't see how any of this affects me."

Sterling stepped closer to her. "Norma Jean said you two used to be friends."

"Fifty years ago maybe."

"Before Cedric."

Marion straightened. "He chose me," she said sternly, "because I made him laugh. No matter what Norma Jean thinks, I didn't steal him from her."

Sterling turned his palms upward, a non-verbal plea for help.

Marion Bardot studied him again. Her expression morphed from stern to concern. "You're serious about this mobster angle? That Norma Jean could really be in danger?"

"Yes."

Marion turned and locked the back door. When she faced him again, she said, "Come here and stand on the mat. You're getting my floor all wet."

They changed positions. Marion grabbed a mop from a nearby bucket and wiped up the water that had dripped from Sterling's clothes. "Have you considered this all may be nothing?" she asked. "Maybe it's a coincidence. Norma Jean could be sick, or perhaps she took a vacation day."

"She would have left a note or called me."

For a moment, perhaps Norma Jean *had* called him after he left his house. He'd have no way of knowing because he wasn't carrying his cell phone. "Do you have Norma Jean's number?" Sterling asked.

Marion set the mop against the wall. "We haven't talked in ages. I've no need for her number."

"What about where she lives? Do you know that?"

"That I do know. Everyone knows where everyone lives in this town." She motioned toward the rear of the store. "Norma Jean's on Apple Street. A few blocks away." Marion waved her hand. "That's not saying much since everyone's a few blocks away in Wandering Springs."

"What about the house number?"

"How would I know?" Marion scoffed. "Go up two blocks to Apple and hang a right. Hers is the only yellow house on the block."

"Thanks," Sterling said. He headed for the door.

"Wait."

He stopped.

"Why are these people looking for Norma Jean?"

"I don't know," Sterling said. "One thing is for sure; they don't want cupcakes."

Marion smirked. "I like them already."

"They're Canadians."

She leaned forward as if waiting for Sterling to say more. When he didn't, she said, "Contrary to what you think, Canadians are nice people."

Sterling grunted his disapproval of her statement.

"Don't be like that. We get lots of business when they cross the border. Their loonies spend as good as American dollars here. Anyone spreading rumors—"

"This isn't a rumor," Sterling interrupted. "Something bad is happening out there."

"Regardless," Marion said, "you should be

careful about lumping these troublemakers in with all Canadians."

Sterling reached for the door.

"Wait," she said again.

He glanced back.

"My offer stands. Come work for a grown-up bakery." She flicked her hand. "There are no sprinkles or gummy bears here. No grubby children licking the frosting from miniature cakes."

At another time, Sterling might have considered the offer. His life was always better when it was free of children. "I've got to go," he said.

"Me, too." Marion eyed her mixing table. "If the Frosty Petal's closed today, I'm going to be extra busy."

The lilt in her voice showed Marion's concern for Norma Jean's absence had quickly vanished.

Sterling slipped out the back and into the alley. His head swiveled as he scanned for the BMW and Lexus.

***

Sterling emerged from the alley like a thief leaving a crime scene. It was a familiar feeling but one with an odd underpinning. He'd done nothing wrong. During his days with the Satan's Dawgs, Sterling's former self had committed crimes and fled under the cover of darkness. He sometimes committed crimes during the day and scuttled from shadow to shadow.

He hurried through the cold rain. Sterling wished he had taken the time to investigate why his car wouldn't start this morning. If it had been a dead battery, perhaps he could have woken a neighbor. Unfortunately, he didn't really know those who lived on either side of him.

Sterling had experienced worse conditions than a dreary morning like this. He just needed to suck it up. Being wet and cold was temporary. He'd be dry and warm soon enough.

He searched for the two luxury cars as he went. Not seeing or hearing either, Sterling turned north. He fought the urge to run just in case the Canadians saw him. His strides remained quick and long, hopefully resembling those of a man homing in on his missing cat.

Sterling didn't call for Travis anymore. There was no need. If one of the sleek sedans reappeared, he certainly could return to his act.

All the homes on this stretch of Apple Street were dark; the residents still apparently snuggled in their beds. Streetlights provided enough illumination for Sterling to make out the coloring of the houses. About halfway down the block, Sterling found a yellow home.

A waist-high white picket fence bordered the front yard, and a mailbox stood guard at the edge of the property. No name was listed on the side of the metal container—only the house number. A row of large arborvitae trees lurked near the house.

Sterling checked in both directions. Nothing

moved in the darkness but him.

The fence's gate squeaked open. Sterling stepped through and closed it behind him.

A pair of headlights lit up the neighborhood as a car pulled onto Apple Street.

Sterling crouched and he darted toward the large trees near the front of the yellow house. He peeked between two of them and watched as the black BMW slowly drove by. It didn't stop at Norma Jean's house.

Rain pelted the house's roof and cold water cascaded over the gutter-less edge, landing on Sterling's crouched form. He didn't dare leave his hiding position even though water poured down his neck, under his jacket, and soaked his shirt.

When the sedan passed, Sterling hurried around the arborvitaes to get away from the roof's waterfall. He remained crouched in the yard, shivering. From where he stood, he couldn't see if the BMW had left the neighborhood. He couldn't hear the engine over the storm.

Blood pounded in Sterling's ears. The BMW might have stopped at the end of the block; its engine quietly idling.

Eventually, Sterling hurried to the picket fence and looked in the direction the BMW had traveled. It was no longer on the block. He spun, trotted along the pathway and bounded the steps to the yellow house. When he rang the doorbell, a soft *bing-bong* sound came from inside.

Passing seconds felt like minutes while Sterling stood on the front porch. He was soaked completely through. He couldn't have been any wetter if he had jumped into a river.

Sterling left the front steps and ran around the side of the house. A detached garage sat near the back alley. He approached the structure and opened a side door. Sterling didn't dare turn on a light and call attention to himself.

Even in the dark, Sterling could tell the car parked inside the garage was Norma Jean's Chevy Bolt. He quietly closed the door and walked across the backyard. He wrapped his arms around himself as protection from the cold rain.

Sterling tapped on the house's rear door. He didn't want to make too much noise. He continued the light rapping, stopping occasionally to whisper, "Norma Jean, it's Sterling."

Eventually, a voice came from the other side of the door. "How do I know it's you?"

"Because if it wasn't," he said, "I'd kick in the door."

A lock slid back, and the door opened. Norma Jean glanced at him, then checked behind him. "What're you doing here, Silver?"

Sterling hugged himself tighter. "There are some Canadians looking for you."

"There are?" she asked, worry crossing her face. "Don't you worry about that. Just take the day off and stay home. I'll call you later." She started to close the door.

"Wait." Sterling lifted a hand as his body shook sharply. "What's going on here?"

Norma Jean's eyes widened. "Silver, you're freezing."

"I'm fine. Tell me what's going on."

"You poor dear," she said, grabbing his arm and pulling him inside. "Let's get you warm."

Chapter 7

A grayness enveloped the kitchen. Courtesy of the ambient light from outside, Sterling could see the sink, refrigerator, and oven as he walked into the kitchen. Once Norma Jean shut the door, however, darkness overwhelmed the room.

"Wait here," Norma Jean said, and she hurried off.

Sterling hugged himself to stop trembling, but it didn't work. Sterling hunched and gritted his teeth, trying desperately to will his mind over his body.

Norma Jean returned and said, "Here." She shoved a large towel into hands. "Take off your coat."

Sterling wrestled the wet garment off his shoulders, awkwardly switching the towel from one hand to the other while he did so. He held the coat in his left hand, but Norma Jean didn't take it from him.

"Is there a place to hang it?" he asked.

"Drop it on the floor. We'll worry about it later."

Sterling's eyes were starting to adapt to the lack of light in the room. He could make out Norma Jean since she stood only a foot or so in front of him. He dropped the jacket and wiped the towel over his head and chest.

"I'm sorry I don't have a change of clothes for you," Norma Jean said. "I've brewed some coffee, however. Would you like some?"

Sterling wanted to know what was going on, but warmth was his top priority. "Coffee sounds great," he said.

Norma Jean opened a cabinet and removed a mug. "Cream and sugar?"

"Black," he said. Sterling dragged the towel over his soaked jeans even though he wasn't sure it would make a difference. "Why are the Canadians looking for you?"

She turned and said, "Here." Norma Jean handed him a cup.

Sterling draped the towel around his neck, took the mug, and immediately sipped it. The coffee warmed his chest, and his shivering lessened.

"Better?" she asked.

He nodded, thankful for the heat radiating from the cup held in both hands. "What's going on?"

"It's okay, Silver, you don't have to worry." Norma Jean tried to sound brave, but her words were heavy with concern. She gently patted his upper arm. "Everything's going to be all right. Go home until I call you."

"I can't do that," Sterling said. "What're you into?"

"I'm not into anything,"

"But the Canadians—"

A noise behind Sterling caused him to turn. Pearl MacKenzie stood at the edge of the kitchen. She clutched a kitchen knife in her fist.

Norma Jean spread her arms wide and stepped in front of Sterling. "You don't need that. It's Silver."

"He might be working with them, eh?"

"Not him," Norma Jean said. "He's harmless." She looked at Sterling. "Tell her you're harmless."

He didn't feel like pretending anymore that morning, especially since the cold, wet clothes sticking to his body were irritating him. "Someone want to tell me what's going on?" His question came out gruffer than expected.

Pearl raised the knife higher. "He doesn't sound so harmless."

Norma Jean stepped closer to Sterling. "Pearl's in trouble."

"He doesn't need to know," Pearl said. "Loose lips sinking ships and all."

"He won't tell a soul." Norma Jean patted his arm again. "Will you, Silver?"

Sterling said, "I know how to keep a secret."

Pearl scoffed. "Not sure I can trust a man who thinks a batch is two."

"He didn't know," Norma Jean said over her shoulder. "Silver's a good guy. Maybe he can help."

"He can't help," Pearl said.

"Why don't you put the knife down," Sterling asked, "and tell me what's going on?"

Pearl tsked. "I need to sit down." She backed away.

"Let's go," Norma Jean whispered. She

grabbed Sterling's elbow and led him into the living room.

He could see better here because some lights along Apple Street bled over the top of the curtains covering the windows.

Pearl dropped into the recliner and put the knife on the coffee table.

"Before you sit," Norma Jean said, "set the towel underneath you."

"I'll stand." Sterling sipped his coffee again. "There are a couple carloads of your countrymen—" Sterling thought about Lark behind the wheel of the white Lexus and corrected his description. "A couple carloads of your countrypeople—" He still didn't like how that sounded so he settled on, "Carloads of Canadians." His lip curled as he said the final word.

"I get the feeling you don't like us," Pearl said.

Norma Jean patted Sterling's shoulder. "Silver likes everyone. He's just cold."

Sterling didn't argue with her. "I want to know why two carloads of mobsters bent on trouble are looking for Norma Jean this morning."

"I should probably sit for this," Norma Jean said. She dropped onto the couch and leaned forward, holding her head in her hands. "How are we going to get out of this?"

"Did you talk with them?" Pearl asked Sterling. "What'd you say?"

"I said I didn't know Norma Jean."

Pearl leaned forward in her chair. Her eyes

narrowed as she studied Sterling. "You lied?"

"I couldn't say I knew her, then refuse their request for help, now could I?"

"Silver's a smart one," Norma Jean muttered. "We can trust him."

"I suppose." Pearl flopped back in her chair.

Norma Jean eyed her friend. "How do you think they know about me?"

"Maybe they've been watching me for a while."

Sterling sipped his coffee. "Why would some mobsters want to keep tabs on you?"

"Could they have followed you?" Pearl asked Sterling.

"Not a chance."

Pearl crossed her arms. "Don't say it like you know what you're doing."

Norma Jean said, "Sterling's in the same situation I am."

"Except he doesn't know anything." Pearl tsked. "Probably should keep it that way."

"Whether you like it or not," Norma Jean said, "you need to tell him what's going on."

"I don't need to tell him anything."

"Either you tell him, Pearl, or I will."

Sterling took another sip of coffee before saying, "You might be surprised what I can understand."

"I'll give you this—" Pearl grabbed the armrests, pulling herself upright to study him. "You don't seem too scared, eh?"

"I wouldn't say that."

"You didn't blink when I pointed the knife at you. Not even a half-step back."

Sterling drank his coffee and watched the two women.

Eventually, Pearl sighed. "I guess if Norma Jean's willing to vouch for you..." Her thought trailed off as her eyes darted toward the Frosty Petal's owner.

"You know I'll vouch for him," Norma Jean said. "How many times do I have to tell you, Silver's a good guy?"

"All right, then." Pearl nervously bit her thumb before saying, "I've got myself in a spot of trouble."

Sterling lifted his chin toward the curtained window. "Who are they?"

Pearl stared at him for several seconds as if still considering whether to speak. Finally, she put her hands on her knees, bracing herself for what was about to come. "They're with the Maple Leaf Mafia."

"You're kidding," Sterling said with a chuckle.

"What's so funny?" Pearl asked, her face tightening with anger. "I'm as serious as a heart attack."

Sterling shrugged a single shoulder. "You gotta admit the Maple Leaf Mafia doesn't sound very intimidating."

Pearl harrumphed. "Seems like they scared you plenty this morning."

"Why not go all out and call themselves the Bacon Brotherhood or the Hockey Hooligans?"

"First of all," Pearl said, "Hockey Hooligans is just stupid. Second, the Bacon Brothers might have something to say about the other name you're suggesting."

"The Bacon Brothers?"

"Heart attack."

"She's telling the truth," Norma Jean said. She slid down the couch to sit closer to her friend. "I've read the news reports about them both."

The existence of the Maple Leaf Mafia and the Bacon Brothers was one more mark Sterling could count against Canada. Crime syndicates should sound scary like The Shadows of Liberty, The Dark Dominion, or The Terrors of Brooklyn. Those gangs evoked anxiety when anyone uttered their names in alleys and back rooms.

The Satan's Dawgs, with the barking horned dog on the back of their leather jackets, instilled fear when rivals mentioned the club.

The Maple Leaf Mafia? It sounded as intimidating as The Lollipop Guild.

"What're they into?" Sterling asked with a smirk. "Trafficking maple syrup across the border?"

Pearl flicked her hand. "What's wrong with you?" She eyed Norma Jean. "What's wrong with him?"

Norma Jean lifted her hands in a calming manner. "Take it easy."

"He's making fun of my situation." Pearl pointed at Sterling. "Don't go making me a part of the Great Maple Syrup Heist, eh?"

"The great what-now?" Sterling asked.

"You don't know nothing." Pearl shook her head. "I knew I should have kept my mouth shut. You're already judging." She frowned. "Just like a citizen."

"I'm a citizen, too," Norma Jean said defensively.

"He probably thinks I'm making this up, being an old lady and all."

Norma Jean scoffed. "We're not old, and Silver doesn't think that. Give him a chance to understand. Don't forget, it took me a minute."

"No matter what I say, he won't believe me." Pearl glared at Sterling. "Will you? I see it in your eyes that you won't."

He set the empty coffee mug on the table. "Try me."

"Try you?" Pearl asked, her voice rising with exasperation. "You wanna know what the Maple Leaf are into, eh? Fine, I'll tell you." She held up her hand and lifted a finger for every item she mentioned. "Drugs, prostitution, fraud." Pearl's recounting of the mafia's list of crimes slowed. "Money laundering, gambling, protection, robbery." She held up seven fingers now. "Uh."

"Murder?"

Pearl lifted another finger. "All sorts of murder. You name it. Murder for revenge, murder for fun, murder for hire."

"That's a lot of murder," Norma Jean said.

"You're telling me," Pearl agreed.

Sterling studied the woman as much as he could in the low light of the living room. "So this Maple Leaf Mafia is real?"

Pearl waved eight fingers at him. "How is this not real?"

"What's with the maple syrup robbery, then?"

"You're focusing on the wrong part." Pearl dropped her hands into her lap. "They weren't even involved in that."

"Just tell me that heist wasn't real," Sterling said.

"I'm not telling you anything more." Pearl eyed her friend. "This guy is gonna get me caught."

Norma Jean patted her friend's knee. "You can trust Silver." She turned to him. "Tell her she can trust you."

Sterling asked, "Why is the mob after you?"

"Why else?" Pearl said. "I talked." As if she needed to clarify who she spoke with, Pearl added, "To the cops."

"You informed?" Sterling asked.

"I ratted." Her lips twisted. "Never in a thousand years would I believe I'd do something like that."

Sterling cocked his head. "And they're what? Trying to get you before it goes to trial?"

"Before?" Pearl's eyes widened. "Kiddo, that ship sailed long ago."

"That horse is out of the barn," Norma Jean agreed.

"That bird has flown." Pearl waggled her hand in the air.

"Meaning?" Sterling asked. "You already testified?"

"Of course, I testified. I was the crown attorney's star witness when they put away Fabrizio Lombardi, the Ottawa Overlord."

"Ottawa?" Sterling had heard of it before but had no idea where it was.

Pearl inhaled sharply. "Oh my Lord." She looked at Norma Jean. "Don't you screen these people before you hire them?"

"Geography isn't a required qualification for the bakery," Norma Jean said.

Sterling asked, "What's the big deal about Ottawa?"

"Ottawa is our capital," Pearl said. "Our Washington D.C."

"I didn't know."

"What do they teach you in school?"

"Not that."

Pearl scoffed. "And the rest of the world looks to you as the world leader."

"Not me," Sterling said.

"Obviously not."

Sterling reached for the mug but remembered it was empty. "About this Fabrizio guy, who was he to the Maple Leaf Mafia?"

"Fabrizio was a boss. He ran the whole east coast." Pearl waved her hand in a big swooping motion. "Nothing happened without his blessing. Not one murder, heist, you name it." She wriggled eight fingers at him again. "If it happened under the banner of the Maple Leafs, it had Fabrizio's backing. Bet your bottom dollar."

"Okay," Sterling said, "I get it. You turned state's evidence on this mob boss. What happened to him?"

"The crown sent him to Millhaven."

Sterling shrugged.

"It's a maximum-security prison in Bath."

He didn't want to ask where Bath was and offend Pearl once more, so he nodded as if he knew.

"Near Toronto," Pearl added.

Her explanation didn't help so he continued to nod.

"Near New York."

"Ah," Sterling said, smiling. "Sure."

"State," Norma Jean said. "Not city."

"Along the border." Sterling chopped the air with his hand. "I get it."

Pearl exhaled sharply. "It's like talking to a dog."

Sterling understood the situation now, but still couldn't comprehend how a cupcake-loving woman in her seventies got involved with the Canadian mob. "What'd you know about Fabrizio that could get him in trouble?"

"I knew everything," Pearl said. "I was his wife."

***

Sterling sat on the couch, nearest Pearl. Norma Jean had gone into the kitchen to make another pot of coffee.

"The cops came to me," Pearl said, "with a recording of Fabrizio talking on the phone, hiring the Halifax Hitman."

He studied her.

"Halifax is the capital of Nova Scotia."

Sterling nodded. "Sure."

"It's on the east coast. You ever look at a map?"

"I know where Halifax is," he lied. "I was thinking about the hitman." Another lie. "What's his name?"

"It's not important." Pearl waved dismissively. "The hitman was arrested along with Fabrizio. They both went to jail, albeit different locations, of course."

"Who was Fabrizio planning to take out?" Sterling asked.

"Take out?" Pearl snickered. "Listen to you. Mr. Tough Guy. Must like the crime shows, huh? Maybe you've read a book or two?"

"Something like that."

Pearl rested her head on the back of the recliner and stared up at the ceiling. "My husband wanted their number one hitter to come for me."

"Your husband wanted to kill you?"

Her eyes cut to Sterling. "Do you need to repeat everything I say?"

Sterling frowned. "I'm still getting up to speed."

"Step on the gas." She motioned toward the kitchen. "Norma Jean picked it up right away."

"So what happened? Did the cops play you a recording of Fabrizio hiring the hitman?"

"That and they showed me the picture of the woman he was seeing behind my back. She was in her fifties with big blond hair and an Instagram account. A real tart, you ask me."

Sterling raised an eyebrow.

"Not sure what upset me more. Her age or the fact that she was a dental hygienist." Pearl clucked. "That woman didn't have an inkling about the life we lived."

"So you turned informer," Sterling prompted.

"I ratted." Pearl snapped her fingers. "Without so much as a second thought." Her hand fell into her lap. "Hell hath no fury and all that jazz."

"Been on the run ever since?"

"Something like that." Pearl leaned forward. "Ever hear of Witness Protection?"

He kept his expression flat. "Canada has a Witness Protection Program?"

"It's real," Pearl said, offended. "Let me assure you."

"You're revealing an awful lot for someone hiding in the program."

Pearl pursed her lips. "I'm stuck on the wrong side of the border. I needed a friend."

He lowered his voice. "You could've lied. You didn't have to tell Norma Jean the truth. You definitely didn't have to tell me."

Sterling felt hypocritical for accusing Norma Jean of violating the rules of the Witness Protection Program. While he hadn't willingly told anyone his true identity, he'd blown more placements than anyone in the history of the U.S. program.

"I couldn't lie to Norma Jean," Pearl said. "Not only is she my friend, but I needed her help. She needed to know what she was getting into."

"Where's your car?"

"I abandoned it on Main Street, near the Frosty Petal."

"Why do that? You could have headed for one of the other crossings. Some operate twenty-four hours, right?"

"They do." Pearl nodded. "However, if the Maple Leafs knew where I was, they'd watch the other crossings, just in case."

"You're sure."

"I'm positive. I know this is hard for someone like you to understand, but I was in the life. I know how they think."

Norma Jean carried a tray as she entered the room. She set it on the coffee table, then handed Pearl and Sterling each a cup. Norma Jean reached for hers but stopped when she noticed Sterling.

"I'll be right back." Norma Jean hurried away.

Sterling sipped his coffee. Before he could take a second, Norma Jean returned with a large blanket. She draped it over his shoulders. Norma Jean collected her cup and moved to the couch, next to Sterling.

He pulled the blanket tighter around him, thankful for the additional warmth. Outside, the rain continued to pelt the house. "How'd you end up at Norma Jean's?" Sterling asked.

"We've had dinner a couple of times," Pearl said. "Once here."

Norma Jean saluted her friend with her mug. "Once at her place in Aldergrove. Beautiful home."

Pearl smiled. "Thank you."

Sterling said, "What happened yesterday between you buying a batch of cupcakes—"

"Four," Pearl said, eyeing her friend. "Can you believe this guy?"

Norma Jean shrugged. "He's new."

"—and two cars full of mobsters cruising our streets."

"I don't know how they found me," Pearl admitted. "They just did. When I returned to Aldergrove, I noticed them watching my house."

"That's when you turned around and headed back for the border?"

"Not right away, no." Pearl shook her head. "I called the Mounties for help."

Norma Jean added, "The Royal Canadian Mounted Police."

"Dudley Do-Right," Sterling said. He remembered the character from the cartoons his grandmother allowed him to watch when he was a child.

Pearl tsked. "This is serious."

"The Mounties couldn't help?" Sterling asked.

"Not fast enough," Pearl said. "I was told to go somewhere safe, and they'd be in touch."

"So you came back to Wandering Springs?"

"It seemed the safest thing to do." She shrugged, then sipped her coffee. "In retrospect, maybe it wasn't."

"Can the Mounties come across the border?" Sterling asked.

Pearl sighed. "Not without some blessing from your government. That's what they told me after I updated them with my position. All that will take time."

"By then," Sterling said, "the sun will be up, and the Maple Leafs will start asking everyone where Norma Jean lives. Sooner or later, someone's bound to tell them."

"Then we're sunk." Norma Jean put her coffee on the table. "Silver and I bake cupcakes, Pearl. How are we supposed to stack up against some professional killers?"

"They're probably not all killers," Pearl said, calmly, "but I get your point. I'll leave before sunup."

"What about the local cops?" Sterling asked. "Have you called them?"

She shook her head. "I wasn't supposed to leave Canada. My handler's trying to deal with this quietly through the official channels and such."

"The Maple Leafs are in town," Sterling said. "The chance for quiet is long gone."

"Then I should call him."

Sterling lifted a hand, a silent signal for Pearl to wait. "What if your handler is in on it?"

"In on what?"

"You left your hometown and crossed the border to evade the Maple Leafs, but they found you here. How do you think that happened?"

"I don't know, but I highly doubt the Mounties were involved."

"Because they're all Dudley Do-Rights?"

Pearl's eyes narrowed. "Point taken." She looked into her coffee cup. "I never should have come here. You're all in danger now."

"It's okay," Norma Jean said, "it's what friends do."

Sterling set his mug on the coffee table and stood. "We need to move."

"Why?" Pearl asked.

"Sooner or later, those goons will find this house. It's just a matter of time."

Norma Jean faced him. "Where should we go, Silver?"

"My house, for starters." Sterling moved to the window to make sure the streets were clear. "We can make a better plan after that."

Pearl remained seated. "This is a bad idea. We should stay here. Hunker down until help arrives."

"I think Silver is right." Norma Jean pointed at the window. "There are killers out there, Pearl. They're asking about me now, which means I get a vote in what we do." She thumbed toward Sterling. "He's been roped into it, too, so he gets a vote. Two to three says we've got to get out of here before they find us."

"How do you know we can trust him?" Pearl asked. "Maybe he'll sell us out the moment we get in the open."

"Sterling's not like that." Norma Jean eyed him questioningly. "Are you?"

"I've been in a couple of scraps," he said.

"Scraps?" Pearl asked. "This won't be a scrap."

"You're safe with me." Sterling tossed the blanket onto the couch. "We'll leave out the back. Get what you need. We're going in a minute."

Pearl reached for the knife.

"Leave it," Sterling said. "No one is dying today."

Chapter 8

The three of them slipped out the back door of Norma Jean's house. The rain continued its frenzied pace and the wind cut through Sterling's jacket.

Living most of his life in Arizona, there was plenty of weather-related misery when the hot and miserable days of summer took root. However, Sterling could often find a building with air-conditioning. At worst, he'd take comfort in some shade. When the summer monsoons hit, they were warm and refreshing. This was miserable.

Hot and sweaty was always preferable to cold and wet.

Sterling glanced over his shoulder. "Stay in the shadows." It sounded grumpy, and he immediately added, "For your safety," in a softer tone. Sterling didn't want Norma Jean or Pearl to bear the weight of his frustrations. Better men didn't do that. They learned how to control their emotions in all situations.

Even on a miserable morning.

Worry creased Pearl's face. The yellow bucket hat she borrowed from Norma Jean protected her hair from the rain. Sterling wouldn't allow her to bring her umbrella since it would attract too much attention. She clutched her red purse to her chest. "I'm gonna say it again: this is a bad idea."

"Better than being a sitting duck," Norma Jean said. Water cascaded over the brim of her Seattle Mariners baseball hat.

"Is it?" Pearl whispered. "We're taking orders from a dishwasher now."

"Silver's a baker's assistant," Norma Jean corrected when they reached the alley. "How will you know when the Mounties are ready to get you?"

"They'll call me."

Sterling stopped and pushed them deeper into the shadows. "You have a cell phone?"

"Of course," Pearl said. "Doesn't everyone?"

"The program let you have one?"

"Why wouldn't they?" Pearl asked. She shrugged before adding, "I mean, it's their phone and all. They guaranteed it was secure."

"Get rid of it," Sterling ordered.

Pearl clutched her purse to her chest. "It's my only lifeline to safety."

"What if I'm right about the Maple Leafs having a mole in the Mounties? Then they can track your phone."

"If that was the case, they would've found me at Norma Jean's."

Sterling shook his head. "Maybe not. Maybe they couldn't track the phone across the border for whatever reason."

Norma Jean's gaze bounced between Sterling and her friend. "Is that true? Can they track your cell phone?"

"They can," Sterling said, "and if the Maple

Leafs don't have a mole inside the Mounties, maybe they've got one inside the phone company. Either way, you should get rid of the phone."

"I'm with Silver," Norma Jean said. "Get rid of it. You can call them from his place."

Reluctantly, Pearl opened her purse and removed her cell phone. She handed it to Sterling. He dropped it to the ground and stomped it with the heel of his boot. The device shattered, sending plastic pieces spiraling across the wet alley. He kicked the broken device into a puddle.

"Couldn't you have just taken the battery out?" Pearl asked.

"No chances," Sterling said. "Let's go."

Pearl looked toward the sky and rain splashed against her cheeks. "We're gonna get soaked. You should have let me bring my umbrella."

Sterling said, "It's one more possibility to make you a target. Cold is preferable to dead."

"Barely," Pearl groused.

He led them west toward his house, hurrying from shadow to shadow. None of the three talked now. The two women breathed heavily as they shuffled to keep up. The sound of their struggling was louder than the falling rain.

Sterling sidestepped a large puddle by moving out of the shadows and into the middle of the alley. Ahead, the black BMW drove north on the nearest street. The car slammed its brakes, and its tires spun as it struggled to race backward on the wet streets.

"Hide," Sterling yelled over the sound of screeching tires.

"What about you?" Norma Jean whispered from the shadows. Panic laced her voice.

"Go," he said without looking at her. "Hurry."

The BMW reversed beyond the alley's entry. Its tires howled in protest as the driver applied the brakes once more. The car's engine whined and it accelerated into the alley. Its headlights washed over Sterling, and he lifted a hand to shield his eyes.

Sterling wasn't going to run and hide. He needed to deal with the fallout here and now. If he ran, the mobsters in the BMW would contact their friends in the Lexus. They'd converge on the area and search for him.

With a second car in this neighborhood, the likelihood the mobsters would also find Pearl or Norma Jean grew exponentially. No, Sterling thought, he needed to stay put in the middle of the alley.

He had to hope the occupants of the BMW didn't contact their counterparts. The luxury sedan didn't race through the alley. Instead, it slowed to an almost leisurely pace. Why hurry when Sterling stood still?

Hopefully, the extra seconds gained from the mobsters' slow approach would allow Pearl and Norma Jean to find adequate places to hide. Sterling fought the desire to look in the direction the two women had run.

Still protecting his eyes from the oncoming

headlights, Sterling waved at the car. He felt foolish for the gesture but believed it was something a citizen might do.

The BMW stopped a few feet from Sterling, and the headlights shut off. The driver and passenger exited the car.

Rain slapped the driver's bald head. He was a trim man with a tailored gray suit. The jacket splayed open, revealing a gun kept in a shoulder holster under his left armpit. His thin black sweater was tucked into his trousers. "Look who it is," he said.

The passenger opened an umbrella. Even though he wore a suit, this one was a sloppy man. The collar of his white shirt was unbuttoned, and his rumpled tie hung loose around his neck. His shoes weren't shiny and one of the laces had come undone. A gun was tucked into his waistband.

Rain pelted the umbrella, providing an out-of-rhythm drumbeat.

"What're you doing?" the driver asked his friend.

"What's your problem?"

"The umbrella." The driver scoffed. "Put it away."

"The boss has one."

"You thinking you're a boss, eh?"

"No," the passenger said. "I guess not."

"You guess not is right. Stow it. We got a job to do."

The passenger frowned as he lowered the umbrella and closed it into its compact form.

"Better?"

"Should never have brought it out in the first place." The driver turned his attention to Sterling. "Find your cat?"

"Not yet." Sterling cocked his head as he pretended to search the nearby shadows. He glanced in the direction he believed Norma Jean and Pearl had fled but didn't see either woman. "He's never been gone this long."

"Yo, buddy." The passenger moved closer to Sterling and poked his shoulder with the small umbrella. "Seen anyone else out in this cruddy weather?"

"Just you."

"Whoa." The passenger smirked. "Check out this guy." He eyed his partner. "You believe this?"

The driver remained several feet away from Sterling. His smile was meant to be disarming but it failed to do so on any level. "What's your name, friend?"

"Why's that important?" Sterling asked. "I'm just looking for my cat."

"Oh my." The sloppy one tapped his chest with the compact umbrella. "The attitude from this one."

"Easy," the driver said, placing a hand on his partner's shoulder. "It's early and we're in an alley." He glanced around. "No one back here but us fellas." His gaze landed on Sterling again and the smile returned. "That's gotta be disconcerting for a fella like you. Am I right?"

Sterling wasn't concerned for himself. He'd

been in a lot worse situations than this. However, he still didn't know where Norma Jean and Pearl were hiding. Maybe they'd gone around one of the houses and to the next street.

Where would they go if they got separated? They hadn't developed a plan in case something happened.

"It's the weather," Sterling finally said. "It's making me irritable."

"See?" the driver said to the sloppy one. "It's the weather."

The passenger waved the closed umbrella. "Wouldn't be so bad if I could use this."

"I'm Declan," the driver said as he tapped his chest. He thumbed toward his partner. "That's Elliott."

"Why'd you tell him our names?" Elliott hissed.

"Because," Declan said with his plastic smile held firmly in place, "that's what friends do." He nodded once, forcefully. "We're all friends here, eh?"

"Right," Elliott said. "Friends." He turned to Sterling, then poked him in the chest with the compact umbrella. "We're friends. Got that?"

"Okay, big guy," Declan said, "Now it's your turn. What's your name?"

"Leaving." Sterling stepped forward as he motioned toward the alley's end. "I'll look for my cat later."

"Hold on, friend." Declan put his hand on Sterling's chest. "We told you our names."

"Yeah," Elliott said, "don't be rude."

"Whatever this is," Sterling said, raising his hands above his shoulders, "I don't want to get involved."

Declan scoffed. "You're already involved, friend. We want to know who you are."

"Yeah," Elliott said, poking Sterling in the chest with the umbrella. "We want to know who you are."

"I already told you; I'm a guy looking for my cat." Sterling lowered his hands slightly. "I want no part of whatever you've got going on."

"Enough," Declan said. He snapped his fingers. "Give us your wallet. Now."

Elliott tapped the umbrella against Sterling's chest again. "Or else."

Sterling grabbed the hand holding the umbrella and punched Elliott in the face. As the sloppy one squealed from surprise, Sterling turned his attention to Declan. He jabbed the driver's nose before following it up with a cross across the driver's chin.

The sudden violence surprised both mobsters and sent them stumbling backward. The men flailed their arms as they struggled to regain their balance.

Sterling pressed his advantage by punching Declan in the stomach and dropping him to his knees.

Elliott tossed the umbrella away and frantically grabbed at the gun tucked in his waistband. Before he could yank it out, Sterling punched him in the elbow. The sloppy man grunted in pain. Sterling threw a roundhouse which connected with the man's jaw. Elliott crumpled sideways onto the ground.

On one knee, Declan desperately reached into his jacket to remove the gun from his shoulder holster. Sterling was too far away to punch the man, so he kicked backward.

He'd never been trained in any martial arts, but Sterling had been in plenty of fights. Everything counted when a donnybrook started. The kick had no style and was off target. He was aiming for Declan's head. Instead, his foot connected with Declan's gun, knocking it away.

The driver looked at his empty hand and searched for where the weapon had landed.

Sterling took one quick step and threw a haymaker. It connected with Declan's temple, knocking the man out instantly.

The fight ended as quickly as it started. Rain continued to fall but Sterling was no longer cold. He inhaled deeply as he watched the fallen men for any movement.

"Wow," Norma Jean said from the shadows.

"We're really in trouble now," Pearl whined.

"Stay there," Sterling said.

He hurried to the black BMW and yanked open the back door. No one was in the rear seat.

A cell phone rang through the car's stereo system. Sterling looked toward the radio's display and saw an international number along with the name *Rhys*. Was that the man in the other car, the one Sterling suspected was an underboss? If so, was he calling to check in on Declan and Elliott? Would Rhys head their direction when he didn't get an answer?

Sterling returned to the two unconscious men, collecting the guns from both. Perhaps he should have checked the trunk to make sure there were no more weapons. He was worried there wouldn't be time if the boss decided to start searching for his men.

Declan and Elliott would be out for another minute or two, but Sterling couldn't account for the occupants of the white Lexus. They could show up at any moment, which meant he needed to hurry.

Sterling moved into the shadows of the neighboring backyard. Norma Jean and Pearl stepped out from behind a small shed.

"That was really something," Norma Jean said. "We saw everything. You're like Chuck Norris." She mimed a karate chop. "A real-life kung-fu master."

Pearl hugged herself. "This is bad." Her body shook as if the cold and rain might be affecting her. Perhaps it was shock. Rain cascaded off her bucket hat and onto her shoulders. "Really bad."

"We've got to go," Sterling said as calmly as possible. He tried to tamp down the adrenaline coursing through his system.

He led the women around the side of the house. Rain beat the lid of a metal trash can. Sterling stopped and tossed the guns into the container.

"What're you doing?" Pearl asked.

"I don't want to be tempted to use them,"

Sterling said, carefully setting the lid back in place.

"I've got no problem with that temptation."

"Who needs guns," Norma Jean asked, "when we've got our own Bruce Lee? Did you see the way Silver kicked the gun out of that guy's hand?"

"Listen," Sterling said, "if we get split up again—"

"Why would we split up?" Pearl asked. Fear laced her question.

"Yeah, Silver." Norma Jean shook her head. "I don't wanna split up. Not now that I know you're a ninja."

"We're not splitting up," Sterling said patiently, "but if it happens, go to Chateau Sweets."

"Is it open?" Pearl asked.

"Not yet, but the owner is baking now."

Norma Jean's brow furrowed. "You want me to go to Marion for help? Not on your life."

"She's the one who told me how to find you," Sterling said. "She knows there's trouble out here."

Pearl's eyes filled with wistfulness. "I could go for a croissant. Maybe it would calm my nerves."

"We're not splitting up," Norma Jean said, "and that's final."

"That's okay," Sterling said, "but we should go."

"So we're not getting croissants?" Pearl asked.

***

Sneaking through a city at night was harder than people imagined. Most municipalities never truly slept. Someone was always awake and in the middle of a work shift. Trash collectors, taxi drivers, and bakers were the least of Sterling's worries when he was a Dawg. Instead, he was concerned with security guards and the police.

This morning, Sterling might have welcomed contact from either of those uniformed personnel. Unfortunately, he remained suspicious of asking anyone for help. It was impossible to tell who could be on the payroll of the Maple Leafs. An American cop taking bribes from the Canadian mob was highly unlikely, but Sterling couldn't dismiss it outright. If he'd learned anything over the past few months, it was to not discount chance.

Sterling stopped at the edge of Birch Road and looked both ways. The rain continued to pour, and large puddles formed along the curbs. Sterling waved for Norma Jean and Pearl to move forward. The two women dashed as fast as they could across the road and into the next alley. They disappeared into the shadows. Sterling lingered to ensure no one had seen them moving.

Security guards usually fell into two categories: overeager cop-wannabes and retired ex-lawmen who didn't know how to stop working. Regardless, they both paid too much attention to elements that really didn't matter. Security guards were unnecessary in Wandering Springs. Restaurants and tourist shops weren't high risk targets. Criminals wouldn't expect a payday if they broke into a bakery, a cupcakery, or a used bookstore. Roving security guards, those paid to check on the homes of the super wealthy, also weren't in this town.

Sterling sprinted across the road and into the alley's shadows. He led Norma Jean and Pearl further west.

Cops, on the other hand, were constant irritants in Sterling's past life. They were always in the wrong place at the wrong time. Whenever the Dawgs pulled a heist, an officer with an inquisitive eye invariably drove by, full of inane questions and unbridled authority. The few times Sterling's former self could have used the help of an honest cop, none were to be found.

Which was like now.

Sterling, Norma Jean, and Pearl scampered through the alley, moving from shadow to shadow. A big dog angrily barked right before it slammed into a tall cedar fence, shaking its planks. The three stopped and Norma Jean gasped. Sterling lightly grabbed her by the arm and pulled her along. The dog continued to snarl.

"Ignore it," Sterling said. "He can't hurt you."

"It will if he eats through the fence."

Being a low-risk crime area, Sterling had seen only one patrol car from the Whatcom County

Sheriff's roll through town since his arrival in Wandering Springs. It never even stopped. The deputy behind the wheel likely had orders to occasionally make his presence known to give the locals a sense of security. Sterling had never seen anyone stopped for a traffic infraction in town, nor had he heard of a single crime occurring in the area.

Sterling slowed at the next road. Norma Jean and Pearl huddled behind him. He glanced in both directions, saw nothing moving, and waved them forward. Behind them, the big dog continued to bark, and a man cried, "Shut your trap!"

Norma Jean trotted across Chestnut Road and into the alley. Pearl, however, remained behind. Rain flowed over the brim of her bucket hat. Her face was pale, and she shivered. "How much further?"

"A few blocks," Sterling said.

She clucked her dissatisfaction but didn't say anything.

"We'll get warm soon."

"Not before we freeze to death," Pearl grumbled, then hurried after Norma Jean.

Sterling didn't move. He stayed at the alley's exit and scanned the road. Hearing an approaching engine was difficult due to the rain and the incessant barking from behind them.

He only worried about the Maple Leafs in the Lexus. Right now, the occupants of the BMW were probably still recovering from their encounter with Sterling.

The big dog continued to bark, and another neighbor joined in the chorus for quiet.

"Stuff it, you mutt!" the second man hollered.

A third man bellowed, "Stop shouting! Some of us are trying to sleep!"

Even from half a block away, the commotion was surprisingly loud given the rainfall. Sound traveled further at night, but Sterling expected the storm to lessen the distance the voices and barking would travel. He was also surprised the men were yelling out their windows during a rainstorm. Perhaps it was Northwestern Washington behavior. Maybe it was just small-town conduct. Heck, it could just be this neighborhood. Regardless, all the yelling caused Sterling some concern because it might bring unwanted attention.

Lights entered the alley behind Sterling and cast a long shadow in front of him. He didn't turn around. He knew immediately who it was— the Maple Leafs in the white Lexus.

"Hide," he called to Pearl and Norma, then Sterling turned and ran toward downtown. His soggy boots slapped the concrete sidewalk.

An engine whined as the Lexus careened into the roadway. Its tires screeched loudly as they struggled for grip on the wet, slippery asphalt. Sterling didn't have to look back to know what was occurring. He'd been chased by plenty of vehicles, many of them driven by cops.

The driver honked once—a long, irritating blare.

Sterling glanced back now as the Lexus

passed him. The driver slammed its brakes, turning the car into a sideways skid. Sterling stopped running and prepared for a confrontation. He wished he had kept one of the guns he lifted off the other Maple Leafs. If he had, he'd most likely use it. Sterling didn't want to be that version of himself ever again.

When the sedan rocked to a stop, the three mobsters exited the vehicle with varying speed.

Lark, the female driver, was the fastest. She was free of the car and around the hood before the other two even stepped foot into the street. Her suit jacket swung open as she stalked toward Sterling. She clutched a gun in one hand while she pointed with the other. "Where do you think you're going?"

Theo also carried a gun, but the man Sterling suspected was named Rhys didn't have a weapon.

"What's the hurry, bub?" Theo asked. Standing now, he was bigger than Sterling first estimated. He stood several inches taller than Lark and almost as tall as Sterling.

Sterling relaxed. He didn't believe these three knew about his fight with Declan and Elliott. Sterling thumbed over his shoulder. "My cat ran this way."

"Still haven't found him, huh?" Rhys was older than the other two by twenty years and thicker in the middle. He wore a knee-length coat over his suit. His hands were empty.

"Like I said," Sterling explained, "I spotted him, and he ran away."

"That doesn't explain," Lark said with a waggle of her gun, "why you were running?"

The continued commotion back in the alley provided Sterling with a convenient excuse. He waved in the direction of the barking. "That dog scared him."

The mobsters cocked their heads, obviously listening to a trio of neighbors now yelling at each other.

"I almost caught him," Sterling lied. He slapped his hands together, then pushed one out in front of him like a rocket taking off. "Then that stupid dog scared him."

Calling the dog stupid wasn't something Sterling would normally do, but he was acting now. Playing up his imaginary frustration would help sell his story. He'd done an excessive amount of acting the past few months to avoid trouble and was beginning to think he was pretty good at it.

Acting, not avoiding trouble. He'd been terrible at staying out of trouble. Standing in the rain while surrounded by three Canadian mobsters proved that.

"Your cat got a name?" Rhys asked.

"Travis."

Lark clucked. "What kind of name is that?"

"Easy," Rhys said. "A man can name his cat whatever he likes."

Sterling considered the underboss. He seemed like an even-tempered sort, the type of guy who would rise high in the corporate world but would peter out in middle management of a criminal enterprise.

Rhys turned the collar up on his coat and hunched his shoulders against the rain. "What kind of cat?"

"Orange," Sterling said.

Theo's nose crinkled. "He didn't ask for the color."

Sterling hoped to extend the conversation. The longer they talked, the further Norma Jean and Pearl could get. Hopefully, the two women would continue to Chateau Sweets as planned in the event they were separated. "I don't know his breed," Sterling said, "He's a mutt."

Rhys smiled in a fatherly way. "Mutts are dogs. Probably like that one." He flicked his hand toward the noisy dog in the alley. "Mixed breed cats are moggies."

"Moggy?" the woman asked as she eyed her leader.

Theo scoffed. "Sounds like one of those wizards from Harry Potter."

While Sterling wanted to waste time, it seemed a strange conversation for them to have at this moment. Not only had they pursued Sterling out of the alley, but this group was still looking for Pearl MacKenzie.

Overhead, thunder rolled.

"That probably scared the little guy, too," Rhys said. "How long's he been gone?"

"About an hour."

"How'd he get out?"

"I heard a noise," Sterling lied. "When I opened the door to investigate, he bolted."

The boss slapped his hands, mimicking Sterling's earlier gesture. "Just like that."

"Just like that," Sterling agreed, believing his acting was really top notch now. Surely, he could join a local troupe. He wondered if Lynden had a theater. If not, maybe the town of Blaine did.

"What do you think?" Rhys eyed his compatriots.

"Guy's a mope," Theo said.

"I don't know." Lark turned her head and spat. "I can't get a good read on him."

"I think," the boss said, "he's a fly in the ointment."

Lark eyed Rhys. "You want I should take him out?"

Sterling raised his hands but remained silent. These three were smarter than Declan and Elliott because they stayed out of striking range. Sterling would have to move closer to them, or he'd have to get them to step forward. Either way, he didn't like the odds. Two guns were in the equation and that meant he was at a significant disadvantage. Sterling kicked himself for throwing away the pistols he took from Declan and Elliott. Maybe the old version of himself wouldn't be so bad right now.

"A nuisance like this," Rhys said, "doesn't need a permanent solution."

"I don't know about that," Lark replied, but she lowered her gun, nonetheless.

Sterling dropped his hands. "Didn't mean to worry you all."

"You couldn't worry us if you tried," Theo said, then eyed his boss. "Can we get out of this rain?"

Lark motioned with her gun toward downtown. "You see a BMW?" the woman asked. "A black one?"

"Earlier," Sterling said. "On Main Street. When they were talking with you."

The boss shoved his hands into his coat and pulled the garment tighter around his body. "If you see our friends, tell them we're looking for them."

"Something happen?" Sterling tried his best to look innocent.

"They're not answering our calls," Rhys said.

"Maybe a cell tower is down because of the storm."

"The phones are working fine. Let's go." The boss jerked his head toward the Lexus and both collaborators hurried back to the sedan.

Theo climbed in quickly and slammed the door behind him. Lark, on the other hand, paused a moment to appraise Sterling once more before climbing into the driver's seat.

"Good luck with your moggy," Rhys said.

"Thank you." Sterling was fully confident that he should try acting. "The little guy is around here somewhere." He was really hamming it up now.

Rhys backpedaled a couple of steps, before turning and slipping into the rear seat of the Lexus.

The white sedan lurched forward which

caused Sterling to hop out of the way. Its engine revved once, and the car sped around the corner.

***

Sterling took his time entering the nearby alley. He didn't want any of his actions to appear anxious just in case the Maple Leafs were watching him from somewhere. When he finally made it into the shadows, he whispered, "Norma Jean? Pearl?"

Not getting an answer, he picked up his pace and continued calling softly for the women.

The situation was more urgent after the second encounter with Rhys, Lark, and Theo. When Elliott and Declan woke from their forced slumber, they'd report to the boss about their altercation with Sterling.

If that happened, all five Maple Leafs would come looking for him. Their search for Norma Jean and Pearl might even be suspended.

Sterling slowed to a shuffle. Maybe that should be his plan. Get the women to safety, then run around causing havoc until the Mounties arrived to whisk Pearl to safety.

It sounded like *Die Hard*, a movie he'd watched years ago in the Satan's Dawgs clubhouse. His plan to avoid the Maple Leafs also reminded him of a couple of run-ins he'd had recently. Once with the mob at a theme park. The other time with a crooked lawman in an out-of-the-way convenience store. If his plans to cause trouble were anything like the *Die Hard* movies, he shouldn't try for a third. He remembered that film not being as good as the earlier versions.

"Norma Jean?" he whispered again. "Pearl?"

Another thought crept into his mind. Perhaps he should call for help. The U.S. Marshals provided him with a hotline if he ever got into a dangerous situation. The number led to a front, a business disguised as something else, in case anyone hostile was ever listening. In the past, the hotline was disguised as a travel agency, a horoscope hotline, and a fish warehouse.

The marshals responded every time he called, since they were dedicated to hiding him. Marshal Krumland, his current witness inspector, threatened to remove him from the Witness Protection Program if Sterling blew another placement. That meant he could be sent back to prison, a fate Sterling wanted to avoid. Krumland said it with such conviction, Sterling believed the man might actually prefer that over his continued involvement in the program.

Sterling stopped moving and listened. He heard nothing except for the continued patter of the rain. Had Norma Jean and Pearl continued to Chateau Sweets like he suggested? If they had, they were likely safe. However, he couldn't assume that, so he continued searching the alley.

His thoughts returned to Marshal Krumland. Maybe the lawman wouldn't throw him in prison. All cops lie, after all. It was a truth Sterling learned on the streets. Why would the marshal lie in this situation if the goal was to keep Sterling from blowing another cover? Maybe Krumland thought prison was worse than the outcome Sterling knew was a real possibility—the marshals could kick him out of the Witness Protection Program.

If that happened, he'd be forced to hide himself. Sterling didn't have the knowledge or the resources to go up against the Satan's Dawgs or the mob. He needed the marshals and the program. It was an unpleasant truth. Was an unprotected life on the outside better than being tossed back in prison? Yes, but only barely. The Dawgs and the mob could get to him in either situation.

"Norma Jean?" Sterling called as softly as the rain allowed. "Pearl?" He trotted toward the end of the alley.

"Psst."

Sterling stopped and looked around. No one moved from the shadows. Three trash cans huddled near a detached garage. "Who's there?" Sterling asked.

Norma Jean rose from behind one of the cans. "Silver, you okay?"

"Where's Pearl?"

"We got split up back there when we heard the car." Norma Jean glanced up and down the alley. Concern washed over her face. "We've got to find her before they do."

Sterling jerked his head. "Let's go."

He stayed in the shadows while he hurried. "Pearl?" he whispered.

"Pearl?" Norma Jean echoed softly. She struggled to keep up with Sterling as evident by her raspy breathing.

He slowed. "We need to get you to safety."

"Not until we find Pearl," Norma Jean protested.

"I'll find her, but we're all in trouble now."

Sterling gently grabbed Norma Jean's arm and led her through an unfenced yard. She didn't protest. They slowed when they neared the next street. Both glanced in opposite directions to ensure no lurking luxury sedans waited. Sterling guided her across the road and into another unfenced yard.

When they made it to the alleyway, they were behind the businesses fronting Main Street. Ahead was the rear of Chateau Sweets.

Sterling headed toward the French bakery, but Norma Jean pulled free of his grip.

"I've changed my mind," she said.

"Why?"

"You know why."

He motioned toward the back door. "It's the only business open."

"I don't care." Norma Jean frowned and crossed her arms. "I'll take my chances out here."

"All right," Sterling said, "if that's what you want, it's your choice."

"Thank you for understanding."

Sterling looked up and down the alley. "Be

forewarned. If the Canadians grab you, they'll torture you until you tell them about Pearl."

Norma jean scoffed. "What can I tell them?" Her expression changed to a mask of defiance. "Pearl ran off. I don't know where."

"They'll torture you until they're sure you're telling the truth."

She blinked. "I'll tell the truth right away. I don't know where she is."

"How will they know? They'll torture you anyway."

Her mask of defiance slipped and was replaced by one of fear. "They'll torture me? For real?"

"It's what they do. They have to make sure you're telling the truth."

Norma Jean's shoulders slumped. "Fine. Whatever." She flicked toward the back of Chateau Sweets. "Who cares what she thinks?"

Sterling said, "This is for the best. Trust me." He trotted to the back of the bakery and lightly tapped on the door. In a moment, it opened, and Marion Bardot stared down at them. "Well, well, look what the cat dragged in."

Chapter 9

Sterling, Norma Jean, and Marion stood inside the kitchen of Chateau Sweets. A thick aroma of baking pastries hung in the air. Soft jazz music played in the background.

"You two are soaked," Marion said.

Water dripped onto the floor from Sterling and Norma Jean. The kitchen was warm for which Sterling was thankful. He couldn't remember ever being this cold.

Norma Jean crossed her arms and her eyes darted about the room in an obvious attempt to catalog every utensil and appliance. She sniffed and her nose crinkled with disdain. "What's that smell?"

Marion tsked. "I'd show you around, but I don't want you trailing water through my kitchen."

"I don't need a tour, thank you very much," Norma Jean snapped, "I've owned a bakery a lot longer than you."

"This isn't a competition," Marion said.

Norma Jean scoffed. "Everything's a competition with you."

Marion sighed. "We used to be friends."

"I don't remember that being the case."

An uncomfortable silence fell between the two women.

Sterling said, "Thank you for your help."

"That's rich," Norma Jean blurted.

Marion frowned. "You don't want my help?"

"We were doing fine without you."

"Then why are you here?"

"Silver is prone to exaggeration."

"In that case," Marion said, motioning toward the door, "I'll see you out."

"I know the way." Norma Jean reached for the doorknob.

Sterling lightly grabbed Norma Jean's arm and turned her around.

"Listen," he said to his boss, "we need Marion's help, like it or not."

"Guess which one I choose?"

Marion crossed her arms. "People in need usually show gratitude to someone willing to help."

"You can take my gratitude and shove it—"

"Norma Jean," Sterling interrupted.

"What?"

"You need to stay here while I find Pearl."

A petulant expression settled on Norma Jean's face. "I can help you look."

"Who's Pearl?" Marion asked.

Norma Jean pointed at her. "She's no one you need to know."

Sterling said, "Pearl's a customer."

"She's a friend," Norma Jean corrected, "but Marion wouldn't remember what it was like to have one of those."

Sterling set his hand on his boss's shoulder. "Pearl's in trouble, and I need to find her."

"Is this about those Canadians asking about

cupcakes?" Marion asked.

"They're with the Canadian mob," Sterling said.

"You're sure?"

"Positive."

Marion pursed her lips. "Huh. Who would have thought?" Then she asked, "What do they want with this Pearl person?"

"To kill her," Norma Jean said. "Us, too." She held her thumb and forefinger like a gun. "Scared yet?"

"They want revenge," Sterling clarified. "Pearl testified against their boss." He didn't see the harm in telling the truth. If Pearl made it safely through this situation and reunited with the Mounties, they'd surely give her a new identity. They'd probably even give her a choice, unlike his experience with the marshals, considering how super nice Canadians supposedly were. Sterling experienced a tickle of either disdain or jealousy. He couldn't tell which.

Marion nodded slowly. "And they figure grabbing Norma Jean will lead them to Pearl?"

"They figured wrong," Norma Jean said. "They couldn't get anything out of me in a million years."

Sterling knew that wasn't true. No one could hold out forever against torture. At some point, everyone breaks. He asked Norma Jean, "You go to the dentist?"

"What kind of question is that at a time like this?"

"Ever have a cavity filled?"

She smirked. "Who hasn't?"

"Imagine it without Novocain."

Norma Jean's face whitened.

"That'd be just the start," Sterling said. "Even if you gave in, they'd keep hurting you because they'd have to make sure you were telling the entire truth."

Norma Jean put her hand on the side of her face and swooned. "I don't feel so good."

Marion directed her to a stool near a steel mixing table. Sterling held Norma Jean's arm until she settled into place.

"Take a deep breath," he said.

Norma Jean inhaled deeply and held it. Her cheeks puffed with air.

"Let it out."

The breath whooshed free.

Marion filled a glass with water and handed it to Norma Jean. "Drink."

With a grateful nod, she accepted the water and sipped it. The color slowly returned to her cheeks.

"You're safe here," Marion said. "If you want, we can ignore each other and not talk about anything."

"I'd like that." Norma Jean sipped once more, then added, "The ignoring each other, that is."

"Then it's settled." Marion turned to Sterling. "I need to finish my morning prep and you need to find a woman."

He nodded. "Don't open this door for anyone."

"Can I open my store?" Marion waved a hand toward the ovens. "If I don't, I'm going to throw away a lot of perfectly good delectables."

Norma Jean grunted into her glass.

"If I don't find Pearl before the sun comes up," Sterling said, "we're going to have bigger problems than wasted treats." He thumbed over his shoulder. "The border will open and more of those mobsters will join the search."

"What about the Mounties?" Norma Jean asked.

He shrugged. "That's a good question."

Sterling headed for the door. He opened it just wide enough to peer into the alley. Finding it clear, he slipped into the morning darkness and pulled the door closed behind him. He ran through the heavy rain and entered the nearest shadow.

***

Sterling wasn't sure how to find Pearl. He wasn't a bloodhound.

While with the Dawgs, Sterling was the club's bookkeeper, the one who dispensed the perverted justice the club demanded. He never really tracked anyone. Instead, that job fell to the club's bloodhound. That man who located the targets and pointed Sterling at them.

Sterling once asked why all the club's coded titles weren't reminiscent of canine breeds. It seemed a natural course of action, after all. The president explained there were too many duties that didn't fall neatly into dog categories. Also, renaming the club's officer positions like president, secretary, or sergeant-at-arms would make the Dawgs a joke.

It's the same reason the Satan's Dawgs didn't officially call their prospects "puppies." No one would respect the club if they did. Some brothers might've referred to newbies as pups, but they never did it within the public's earshot.

Sterling trotted through the shadows and called, "Pearl." Every now and then, he'd stop and listen. The rain made hearing anything difficult. "Pearl," he called again, then darted across a street and into the safety of an alley.

Lights were on in a couple of houses now. Not many, but enough that Sterling was aware. The town would stir from its collective slumber soon. Wandering Springs' older residents would likely be up before the sun broke the horizon. Sterling didn't worry too much about the other citizens running afoul of the Maple Leafs. The mobsters did not want witnesses, especially while they were in the United States.

However, Sterling couldn't imagine the Canadians giving up easily and returning home. They came this far and had Pearl cornered in a small town. Quitting wouldn't be an option.

What would they do if they found her?

Thinking about the situation from their perspective, Sterling believed the Maple Leaf crew had two options. First, they could kidnap Pearl and slip her into a trunk. Then they'd drive her across the border and deliver her to the big boss.

That scenario was rife with risk. An

inquisitive border guard could ask to look in the trunk. Their kidnapping plan was sunk if they were discovered at the border. The Maple Leafs could attempt to flee but they'd be quickly caught. Sterling wasn't a fan of Canada, but he had to admit an entire country's police force would be daunting to elude.

Which left the second option as the most viable—kill Pearl right here in Wandering Springs.

This wasn't a perfect plan either. The Maple Leafs were in a foreign country, albeit right across the border from their own. If their involvement in the murder was discovered after they managed to flee back into the Great White North, the mobsters would still have trouble. Canada had an extradition agreement with the United States.

"Pearl," Sterling whispered as he left the alley's shadows and darted across the next street. He slowed to a jog as he entered the darkness of another alley. "Pearl," he called out again.

Looking for the missing woman was like searching for a needle in a haystack. She could be anywhere. Why didn't she go straight for Chateau Sweets like Sterling suggested? Besides the Frosty Petal, how much time had Pearl spent in Wandering Springs? Perhaps she got turned around and was lost. He doubted that. It wouldn't take anyone very long to determine where they were in the small town. All they had to do was find where downtown was to reorient themselves.

A dreadful thought occurred to Sterling then. Perhaps the Maple Leafs had already found Pearl and they wrapped up their deadly business. Sterling shook the terrible notion from his head. He couldn't think like that. He had to remain hopeful.

Maybe the mobsters stopped her from heading toward the French bakery. If she saw one of their cars, Pearl might have fled in a different direction. She saw the black BMW when Sterling fought with its two occupants in the alley, but had she seen the white Lexus? In the end, it didn't matter since Pearl was gone. The most important question was where would she hide in Wandering Springs?

Pearl knew where Norma Jean lived but she wouldn't go back there because the Maple Leafs might discover the house at any moment. She also wouldn't go to Frosty Petal since the mobsters first asked about the cupcakery.

That left Chateau Sweets.

Perhaps Pearl went there after all but simply took more time to arrive than Sterling and Norma Jean.

He slowed to a walk and looked over his shoulder. Sterling couldn't see the rear of Chateau Sweets anymore since he was blocks away. Nothing else moved in the alley.

Sterling still didn't have his phone so he couldn't call anyone to find out if Pearl had shown up. Not carrying the device usually came with no downside. Unfortunately, this moment was forcing Sterling to reconsider that decision. Although, if he had the phone with him now, it wouldn't do him any good. He didn't know the number to Chateau Sweets, and Norma Jean's number was written on a notepad in his kitchen.

Sterling contemplated returning to the French bakery, getting warm, then heading to his house for a dry set of clothes. Before he could consider a change in plans any further, lights filled the alleyway behind him, and he spun.

The headlight configuration was uniquely BMW. The vehicle's engine roared as it sped through the alley, bumping and careening over potholes.

Sterling had only a second to decide a course of action. He hopped on a metal trash can. The container made a horrible racket as it banged into the nearby cedar fence. Sterling briefly stabilized himself before jumping over. He landed in a children's pool half-filled with rainwater. His feet slipped out from underneath him and he flopped onto his back with his arms spread wide. Water sloshed over his belly. The back of his head smacked the hard plastic side of the pool.

On the other side of the fence, the BMW screeched to a stop. A car door opened, then quickly closed. The car's engine roared again as it raced away.

Sterling rolled out of the pool onto a mushy lawn. Without looking back, he hastily crawled away. Muddy grass squished between his fingers and his knees sunk into the lawn as he fought to regain his footing.

The trash container clattered against the fence as if someone else jumped on it. "Stop, you!" Elliott hollered.

Sterling, back on his feet now, darted toward the gate leading to the front of the yard. He hunched, expecting a gunshot at any moment, even though he'd tossed Declan's and Elliott's guns into a trash can earlier. A shot never came, and Sterling banged against the gate, causing it to open violently.

Headlights rounded the corner as the BMW's tires squealed for purchase. Its back end swung wildly on the wet street, and the car appeared headed for a large pine tree.

Sterling sprinted across the street, no longer concerned about staying in the shadows. He leaped over a short, white picket fence and entered the front yard of a small white rancher.

A horrible crunch erupted behind him.

Sterling slowed briefly to witness the aftermath. The BMW had hit the tree. Its hood was crumpled, and steam rose from its engine.

Footsteps thudded behind Sterling.

Elliott lumbered into the street. He leaned forward in an awkward gait, his feet struggled to keep up with his shoulders. "Stop," he wheezed.

Sterling didn't obey the mobster's command. Once more, he ran. However, Sterling took the unexpected course of sprinting back at the oncoming man.

Elliott pulled up suddenly and raised his hands in surrender. He only had enough time to mutter a confused, "Hey!"

Sterling never played football in high school nor at any other level. Regardless, he lowered his shoulder and hit Elliott in the sternum, lifting the mobster off his feet and driving him into the ground like a linebacker smacking a quarterback.

Elliott loudly grunted a moment before his head smacked the asphalt. The man's arms collapsed to the ground, and he didn't move.

Sterling didn't want to kill the man. He only wanted to incapacitate the mobster until he could get away. He slapped Elliott's face to get a response, but there was none.

"Get off him!" Declan shouted as he moved around the disabled car. He hurried in Sterling's direction. "I'm gonna kill you!"

The rain sliced through the streetlights.

Sterling stood and faced the approaching mobster.

Declan slowed. "Not gonna happen." He held his fists near his head and bounced on his toes. "I'm ready for you this time."

Sterling didn't want to hang around in the open too long. The Lexus with the other Maple Leafs might show up at any time and he knew they still had guns. If that happened, Sterling's chances of evasion would worsen considerably. He needed to end the fight quickly. He lifted his hands as he neared Declan.

The mobster jabbed hard with his left hand, but Sterling didn't flinch. Instead, he lowered his chin and let Declan punch him in the crown of his head. Declan howled as he pulled his injured hand back.

Sterling seized the advantage and punched the man in the nose. The mobster stumbled backward, his arms rising to protect his face. Sterling slipped to the side and slugged Declan in the belly about where his liver should be.

Declan winced and dropped to his knees. His body contorted in obvious pain, and he tucked his elbows around his midsection. The mobster's head was now unprotected. Sterling hooked a punch that clipped Declan on the chin. The Maple Leaf briefly stiffened before collapsing onto the wet street.

Sterling glanced around, then darted for the closest yard. Worried the noise of the collision would attract the attention of citizens and the other Maple Leafs, Sterling ran farther away from Chateau Sweets. He sprinted through alleys, dashed through yards, and desperately tried to stay among the shadows.

For a moment, the cold vanished. He knew it would only last as long as he kept moving so Sterling ran to the one place he could get warm and not bring danger to Norma Jean or Pearl.

Chapter 10

Sterling stepped into his house and locked the door behind him.

Travis ambled into the living room and flopped lazily onto his side.

"Must be nice," Sterling said.

He slipped off his wet coat and let it fall to the floor before peeling his shirt off. Falling into the kiddie pool left Sterling feeling like a full sponge. He dropped the T-shirt on top of the coat at his feet.

Travis hopped up and wandered over.

"Better not," Sterling said. "I'm soaked."

The tom didn't listen and rubbed against Sterling's dripping pant leg. A moment later, he bounced off as if electrocuted.

"Told you."

A few feet away, Travis executed a perfect figure-eight as he seemingly considered what he'd just experienced.

Sterling knelt and untied his boots. While he did that, the cat returned. He carefully touched his nose against the hem of Sterling's jeans. Finding evidence of wetness, Travis darted out of the room.

"Tough guy," Sterling said.

He kicked off his boots, before tugging off his jeans.

Naked and freezing, Sterling hurried to the

bathroom. He thought about taking a long, hot shower, but he didn't have the time. Instead, he grabbed a towel and dried himself. He thought about combing his wet hair but decided it didn't matter. Sterling ran his fingers through his short mane and called it good.

Next, he hurried into the bedroom and got dressed. Dry jeans and a long-sleeved T-shirt felt great, but it was the socks that really did the trick. The cold vanished as he laced up a dry pair of boots.

Travis wandered into the room to see what Sterling was doing. The cat's actions were casual, as if he had no interest whatsoever in Sterling, especially after the incident with the wet pant leg. Travis paused long enough to consider Sterling's different footwear and bolted into the bathroom.

Sterling lifted the pillow from the head of his bed and grabbed his flip phone.

Travis quickly returned from the bathroom. He seemed to study Sterling. Maybe the cat was even judging him. It was hard to tell with the tom.

"Keep it down," Sterling muttered, "I'm making a call."

With his thumb, he flipped open the phone. Its digital screen illuminated but he didn't dial a number. Not yet at least.

His life wasn't in danger. His cover wasn't at risk of being exposed. If he wanted, Sterling could stay in his house until the afternoon, read his book, and pretend this morning's activities never occurred. His new identity would remain intact, and he could go about his life.

That was assuming the Maple Leafs would forgive the two fights he had with Declan and Elliott. They were low-level thugs so maybe it wouldn't matter. Had Sterling fought with Rhys, the Canadian mob surely would never forgive his involvement.

The Maple Leafs also wouldn't forget about Pearl. They'd find her sooner or later in Wandering Springs and exact the justice they saved for a rat. Sterling's lip curled. He was a rat, too. He knew precisely what lay in store for Pearl if the Canadian mobsters found her.

Pretending to ignore what was happening outside didn't feel good to Sterling. It wasn't what a better man would do. His thumb moved over the keypad, and he dialed the number he'd committed to memory.

It rang three times before it was answered by a groggy male voice. "Krumland."

"It's me," Sterling said.

The lawman cleared his throat. "This better be good."

"You're answering the calls now?"

"Your number is forwarded to my cell."

"No front?"

Lester Krumland scoffed. "Not for you, Beau. Not anymore."

Sterling stiffened. He didn't like the marshal casually using his real name on an unsecured line. Maybe the lawman forgot his operational security because he was still in bed. Perhaps he didn't care.

The lawman sighed. "All right. Let's hear it. What'd you do?"

"Nothing," Sterling said defensively. "I didn't do anything."

"Then why the call?" The marshal grunted. It sounded as if he were shifting his position, perhaps sitting up. "You lonely?" he asked, his voice now sounding normal. "Need a friend?"

"A woman's in trouble."

"Call the police."

Sterling said, "She's Canadian."

"So? She speaks English, right?"

"She's in the program."

"Hold on," Krumland said, his tone suddenly becoming sharp. "How do you know she's in the program?"

"She told me."

"She what now?" The lawman clicked his tongue against the back of his teeth. "She violated protocol?"

"She had to."

Krumland didn't give Sterling a chance to explain further. "I sent you to the farthest reaches of the lower forty-eight and you meet a woman who *claims* she's in the program?"

"I believe her."

"I believe in the Easter Bunny. Doesn't make it true."

Sterling rolled his eyes. "She needs my help."

"Why?"

"Some men are after her."

Krumland scoffed again. "What men?"

"The Maple Leaf Mafia."

"Hold on. You're talking about the Canadian mob. She's in the Canadian program?"

"That's what I'm saying."

"You didn't say that," Krumland said. "You said she was in the program which any reasoning person would assume is ours."

"Do we have Canadians in our program?"

"I'm not answering that," the marshal snapped. "What's this woman's name?"

"Pearl MacKenzie."

It sounded as if Krumland was rummaging through a desk. "Is that her real name?"

"I'd imagine not."

"How'd you meet her?"

"She came into the store."

Krumland stopped making noise. "To buy a cupcake?"

"A batch." Sterling wriggled his fingers. "Which I guess is more than four."

"This Pearl woman revealed she was in the program and the mob was after her all while buying cupcakes?"

"No," Sterling said. "I found out this morning when they stopped me."

"They?" Krumland's voice darkened.

"The Maple Leafs."

"You had contact with the Canadian mob?"

"It wasn't on purpose."

"They know about you?"

"Not exactly," Sterling said.

"What does that mean?"

"They don't know about my program status if

that's what you're asking."

"That's what I'm asking. Why'd they contact you?"

"They were looking for Norma Jean."

Krumland fell silent for a moment as if he was trying to recall who Norma Jean was.

Sterling said, "My boss."

"I know," the marshal grumbled.

"She and Pearl are friends."

"And the Maple Leafs figured that out?"

"Somehow. Yes."

Travis moved closer to Sterling before sitting. He watched Sterling with curiosity.

Krumland slowly exhaled. It sounded like air leaking from a tire. "Are you in danger?"

"You can say that."

"No, Beau, I want you to say it. Are you in danger?"

"Yes."

"How'd that happen?"

"I fought with a couple of them."

"I should've guessed. How many are there?"

"Five in two cars," Sterling said. "Four goons and an underboss. Declan, Elliott, Lark, Theo, and Rhys."

"How do you know their names?"

"It's been a busy morning."

Krumland groaned. "Of course it has."

"Are you going to help me or not?"

"What do you think?"

"If I knew, I wouldn't ask."

Krumland tsked. "I'll make some calls. Until then, are you somewhere safe?"

"I'm at my house but I can't stay here."

"Why not?"

"Pearl's missing."

"This keeps getting better," the marshal said. "Where is she?"

"If I knew that, she wouldn't be missing."

"Okay, seriously. Call the police. Get them involved right now."

"Can we trust them?"

"They're the police," Krumland said with exasperation.

Sterling's upper lip curled, but he didn't respond.

Cops, regardless of local or federal level, insisted their entire profession was filled with righteous and incorruptible individuals. In Sterling's experience, that simply wasn't true. In the past, he'd been unfairly judged by the cops because of his long hair, his size, and the leather jacket he wore. The Dawgs weren't upstanding citizens, but the constitution insisted people were innocent until proven guilty. The police trampled daily on the idea of presumed innocence.

However...

Sterling relaxed his upper lip.

He had developed a fondness for the FBI man who arrested him and got him out of the Satan's Dawgs. Sterling also grew to like his first two witness inspectors. He even met a few competent cops during his previous placements. Maybe he was unfairly judging the cops in the same way they had him.

Sterling shrugged even though the marshal couldn't see the gesture. "Fine. I'll call them."

"On second thought," Krumland said. "Don't."

"How's that?"

"Your identity is still intact. I'm assuming, anyway."

"It's still intact," Sterling said.

"In that case, stay out of it." Krumland tapped something on his end of the call. Perhaps a pen on a desk? "I'll contact my counterparts in the Mounties and alert them."

"Pearl said she already did that."

"Then I'll confirm they're mobilizing for her."

"The border crossing will open soon."

"Good point," Krumland said, "Maybe the Maple Leaf Mafia has some reinforcements coming in. I'll get on this."

"Thank you."

"Beau," the marshal said, "you made the right choice by calling before you got involved too deeply. We can take care of this. Everything will be fine."

"All right."

"But stand down," the marshal demanded. "Stay out of this mess and keep your cover identity intact."

"I heard you," Sterling said.

"Let us do our jobs. Tomorrow, you can go about living your life like none of this ever happened."

Travis stood a couple of feet away from Sterling and continued to watch him. Sterling believed the cat was incapable of forming an opinion, but it sure felt like that's what was happening. Travis didn't look away, didn't flop, and didn't clean himself. The tom resembled a statue—an orange effigy to judgement.

Krumland clucked. "You're not going to stand by, are you?"

"I can't."

"This is why you end up with the problems you get."

"Pearl's a seventy-something woman in trouble. What if it were my grandmother?" Sterling said. "I've got to help. I'll contact you after I find her and get her to safety."

He ended the call before the marshal could protest any further.

Travis watched him for a second more before darting out of the room.

***

The rain fell harder now. At least, that's how it seemed.

Sterling's jacket was wet inside and out, but it was the only one he had. He was a man of simple means who never in his life needed a second coat. Sterling wished he still had his leather jacket from his time with the Dawgs. It would provide far more protection from the rain and cold.

Big raindrops splashed in puddles, a constant pitter-patter which covered the sound of Sterling's movements. He trotted through an alley, calling for Pearl. As he hurried, Sterling listened for the sound of engines and looked for approaching headlights.

"Pearl," he shouted.

The increased downfall muffled most of his concern. He'd heard a forecaster refer to torrential rain before. This had to be what she meant.

Sterling's boots slapped the ground as he ran, creating small explosions of water. He hopped over puddles, hoping to keep this pair of boots dry as long as possible.

A small dog yapped near a chain link fence as Sterling passed. Its white fur was matted because of the rain. The dog bounced with each of its shrill barks. The back door flung open, and an interior light lit up a woman in a housecoat. "Muffin," she hollered. "Get in here!"

Ahead, the white Lexus zoomed by the alley's mouth. Its tires screeched. Sterling stopped, expecting the car to reverse, but it didn't. The engine revved and faded slightly in the distance.

One thought came to mind: the Maple Leafs must have found Pearl. He sprinted toward the alley's end and turned to follow the sedan. Down the street, the sound of skidding tires filled the morning air. Sterling ran toward the sound, turning onto Plum Street.

He immediately realized his mistake.

Down the street, Declan and Elliott huddled near the front end of the crumpled black BMW. The Lexus's headlights shone on the two thugs as they stood in the falling rain. Elliott rubbed the back of his head as Declan appeared to console him by patting his shoulder.

Theo approached the two men, motioning toward the black sedan.

Lark and the boss stayed in the Lexus. Its brake lights blazed bright red in the morning darkness.

Elliott looked at Theo and noticed Sterling. "It's him!" he hollered and pointed.

The rear lights on the white Lexus switched from red to white as the tires spun in reverse, desperately seeking grip on the wet ground.

Sterling bolted into the nearest yard.

"Stop!" one of the men yelled. Sterling didn't look back to discern who said it.

A cedar fence surrounded the backyard. Sterling grabbed its top, scrambled up, and tossed himself over. He landed on a pile of chopped wood. The logs gave way and Sterling crashed to the ground. He got to his feet, stepped awkwardly on a piece of wood, and twisted his ankle.

Sterling grimaced as he hobbled across the wet lawn.

Tires shrieked nearby just before an engine roared again. A car bounced into the alley, its headlights lighting up the dark pathway. Certainly someone was following him on foot, too.

Sterling still had options. He could go right or left and enter another neighbor's backyard. He turned left and jumped onto the cedar fence. His ankle protested as he propelled himself up.

When he reached the top, Sterling had only a moment to realize it looked like he was about to jump into a black hole.

He leaped and his feet hit a trampoline. Sterling's body collapsed on itself and his jaw smacked into his folded knees. The trampoline bounced him away, tossing him onto the soppy grass. Like a man stealing second base, he slid several feet on his belly.

In the alley, a car door opened and quickly closed. "When I find you," Lark yelled, "I'm gonna shoot you in the face."

Sterling had no doubt her threat was true. Of the four soldiers he'd met this morning, she seemed the most capable. He forced himself to his feet and was rewarded with his ankle howling in pain.

"He's not here," Theo shouted from behind the other side of the fence.

"Check the neighbors," Lark ordered.

A light in the nearby house flicked on and a woman peered out a window. Sterling scurried as quickly as he could toward the front yard, banging through the gate as he went.

Elliott stood on the sidewalk, his hand still holding his head. Declan examined the damage to the front of their car. Both men turned in Sterling's direction when they heard the gate bang open.

Sterling ignored the pain in his ankle as he headed straight for the nearest man.

"Please," Elliott whimpered just before Sterling slammed his shoulder into him.

It wasn't a clean hit like the earlier tackle Sterling had made. However, the collision was enough to spin the thug like an unbalanced top. Elliott held his arms out to the side as he tried to stabilize himself. It didn't work. The mobster wobbled into the street where he eventually collapsed.

"You," was all Declan said as he swung at Sterling.

It was a roundhouse, a clumsy strike to start a fight. Sterling ducked it and punched the man in the stomach, doubling him over and dropping Declan to his knees.

Had he more time, Sterling would have liked to hit both men once more, just for good measure. However, Theo and Lark were now chasing him, and those two still had their guns.

Sterling limped across the street, taking long jumping strides on his good ankle. He entered a yard with no fence and continued to the next alley. He stayed in the shadows, prepared to run at the first hint of danger. When he passed an old pickup parked underneath a carport, a woman called, "Hey!"

He instinctively hunched and turned back, expecting to see Lark with a gun clutched in her fist.

Instead, Pearl MacKenzie peered out from the safety of a plastic tarp in the back of a truck bed.

"Where've you been?" she asked, relief spreading across her face.

Chapter 11

The tarp slid from Pearl's shoulders as she started to stand in the truck bed, but Sterling stopped her.

"Stay down," he whispered. "The Maple Leafs are on the next block."

Rain pelted the carport's metal roof. Underneath the shelter was like standing inside a tin drum.

Pearl lowered herself until only her eyes appeared above the truck's rear panel. Her eyes darted left and right. "Are they following you?"

"I think I lost them."

"You think?" Pearl dropped onto her back and pulled the tarp to her chin. "This isn't good."

Sterling leaned closer to Pearl. "How long have you been here?"

"A while now," Pearl said. "After we got separated, I thought I was heading toward the French bakery until I saw a car and hid. When I started walking again, I got myself turned around." She shifted her position. "They don't make these truck beds for comfort, do they?"

"No," he said, scanning the nearby road for anyone moving in the dark.

Pearl grunted as she rose onto her elbow. "I could have figured it out with enough time, but I was tired of getting wet. I thought hiding out here for a while wasn't so bad."

Sterling understood. Even this small break from the rain was playing havoc with his reasoning. He thought about asking her to scoot over so he could hide in the truck bed, too. He wouldn't be warmer, but getting dry was half the battle right now. However, he didn't want to be caught lying down. Better to be on his feet, ready to fight if the Maple Leafs showed up.

Pearl asked, "Where's Norma Jean?"

"At Chateau Sweets."

"Lucky girl. I bet she's in heaven right now. Warm and dry with all those treats to nosh on." Pearl's eyelids drooped and she moaned as if appreciating the taste of a French pastry. When her eyes opened, she said, "Okay, I'm sold." Pearl grabbed the side of the truck and started to pull herself out. "Let's go."

Sterling held up a hand to stop her. "Stay there."

Pearl's expression soured. "Why?"

"The Maple Leafs might still be nearby." He waved in the direction from which he'd come.

"Did they see you?"

"Unfortunately." Sterling patted the truck. "This is a great place to hide."

"I'm cold and wet."

"Better than the alternative."

Pearl smirked. "I'm not the delicate flower you think I am."

Sterling didn't think of her as delicate or a flower.

"Just because I'm old doesn't mean I'm scared." She glanced around the neighborhood.

"Stay here until help arrives."

"How will they know how to find me?"

"I'll make sure they do," Sterling said.

"No. I don't want to hide here. I want to go to the bakery."

"Getting there won't be easy."

"I'm going, with you or without you, and that's the end of that. I could really go for a pastry about now."

Pearl rose to her feet but remained hunched as if to limit the chance of being seen. Sterling helped her out of the truck bed. When her feet touched the ground, Pearl brushed herself off. He shuffled back to give her some room and felt the pain in his ankle again.

"See?" she said. "I can take care of myself."

"Ready?"

"Do you think they'll have a *pain au chocolat*?"

Sterling had no idea what she was talking about. He pointed in the direction of Main Street. "If anything happens—"

"Nothing's going to happen," Pearl interrupted, grabbing his arm.

"But if we get separated again."

"I'm not letting that happen." Her fingers clung to Sterling's bicep. "Especially since we've got extra motivation now—pastries."

Sterling thought living through the morning was motivation enough, but if Pearl needed fresh-baked goodies to help her survive, so be it.

The two entered the rain and headed in the opposite direction from which Sterling had approached minutes before. He figured on taking the long way back to Chateau Sweets, giving the Canadian mob as wide a berth as possible.

Sterling's head swiveled as he limped, looking for the white Lexus or anyone on foot. He didn't like being on the sidewalk. Streetlights provided too much illumination, and the only shadows cast were from the occasional tree. He and Pearl needed to get into an alley as soon as possible.

They found a house without a fence and turned south by cutting through the lawn. A few lights were on inside, but no one appeared to be moving. Sterling bent as he crept underneath the windows. It hurt his ankle, but temporary pain was better than being discovered. He glanced over his shoulder to see Pearl hunching as she walked.

In a moment, they were in an alley and its protective shadows. Sterling led them another block east, farther away from the French bakery. Heavy raindrops splashed in potholes and the rhythm of the storm played on trash can lids. Sterling glanced back at Pearl. She hugged herself as her face trembled.

"Doing okay?" he asked.

"Better than you I suppose," she said. "What happened to your ankle?"

"I twisted it. Won't be much longer."

"I get the feeling," Pearl said through chattering teeth, "we're going the wrong way."

"We're giving the Maple Leafs plenty of respect."

They exited the alley and went south once more. They were two blocks from Main Street now. Sterling didn't know exactly how far they were from Chateau Sweets, but it wouldn't take long to cover the distance. Nothing in Wandering Springs was far.

Sterling led them to the next alley. Just as they were about to enter, the white Lexus turned off Main Street, its headlights swinging onto the side road.

"They found us," Sterling said without looking back. "Hide!"

"Not again," Pearl cried.

Sterling ran in the opposite direction with an awkward hopping gait. He hoped his sudden movement would trigger the chase instinct in the Maple Leafs. It was a tactic the Satan's Dawgs developed after hearing an older cop admonish a rookie for chasing after one of Sterling's former brothers.

"Why are you running?" the older cop had asked.

"I don't know," the rookie said. "The guy ran, so I chased him. It seemed natural."

Separating from Pearl was a calculated risk. The Maple Leafs had chased him twice now. Hopefully, the instinct remained. If they saw Pearl and went after her, Sterling would turn around and deal with them. Ambushes were also a tactic used by his old club.

His boots slapped the uneven ground as he sprinted through the alley. Headlights shone brightly behind him and cast his elongated shadow ahead of him. Sterling almost shouted with joy that the mobsters had followed him as hoped

Then his foot with the hurt ankle caught in a pothole, and he stumbled. His arms windmilled as he struggled for balance. Sterling Carter lost the battle to remain upright, and he careened to the wet ground. Pebbles tore into his palms and his knees raked across the jagged terrain. His head smacked the compacted dirt, and the world erupted with a bright flash and sharp ringing.

The Lexus raced up and skidded to a stop, nearly on top of Sterling.

He shakily pushed himself to one knee, then wobbled as he stood. Sterling took one unsure step when the doors to the sedan opened.

"Run and I'll shoot," Lark ordered.

Sterling stopped, almost thankful for the demand to remain still. He blinked repeatedly as he fought to clear his vision and decrease the ringing in his ears. Sterling lifted his hands in the air, higher than necessary, but he was feeling especially vulnerable right now. He slowly spun around and looked into the bright headlights. He didn't turn away. Instead, he lowered his eyes and felt the rain on the back of his neck.

"Let's just shoot him," Theo suggested.

Another door opened and Rhys stepped out. "Nobody's killing him. Not yet at least."

The boss walked over with more confidence than he should have in this situation. Had the man known Sterling's former role with the Satan's Dawgs, he'd be careful. He certainly would take his hands out of his coat pockets and not leave himself so defenseless.

Unfortunately for Sterling, he swooned as lightheadedness overwhelmed him. Nausea rose from his stomach and into his throat. He tasted bile. Had he given himself a concussion by smacking his head onto the ground?

Rhys studied him as his right hand came free from his pocket. "Not feeling well?"

"Feeling fine," Sterling lied.

"Gonna play nice?"

Sterling blinked with considerable effort. He had trouble focusing on the mobsters but was certain Theo and Lark both held guns. A part of him knew he needed to buy time to clear his head so he could escape, but all he could think to say was, "Lemme explain." The words felt like cotton in his mouth and sounded strange under the ringing in his ears.

"I'll take that as a no," Rhys said.

The boss casually flicked his hand, and Theo smacked the barrel of his gun across Sterling's temple.

Sterling's legs turned to jelly, and he crumpled to the wet ground. He fought to hold onto consciousness as the boss's shadow loomed over him.

"What should we do with him?" Lark asked.

"Put him in the trunk," Rhys ordered. "Maybe he'll answer some questions after he's had a nap."

Sterling slipped into murky darkness.

***

Sterling regained awareness in the tight confines of a trunk. He lay on his side with his knees smooshed into his chest and his head pressed against the wall of the car. His temple throbbed with every heartbeat.

At least he was dry.

His grandmother used to say every cloud had a silver lining. Being out of the rain was the only bright side this situation had.

Then the car moved and violently bounced when it hit a pothole. Sterling was tossed like a ragdoll, and his head smacked the inside of the trunk lid. His world exploded with bright light again, and the ringing in his ears intensified.

It appeared this cloud with a silver lining was part of a bigger storm.

The Lexus slammed into a second and third pothole. Sterling tried to support himself against the sides of the trunk, to stop being thrown about, but it was for naught. His contorted body banged repeatedly into the trunk's ceiling before rebounding to its floor.

He groaned.

Perhaps he should have fought with the Maple Leafs' back in the alley. He was in no condition to win and surely would have been shot by Lark and Theo. He couldn't outrun them either due to his twisted ankle and the concussion he was now certain he had. He wasn't afraid of dying, but Sterling didn't want to go out being shot in the back.

The car bounced again before turning. Sterling didn't try to determine where they were going. The Maple Leafs were still looking for Pearl, which meant they'd hang around Wandering Springs a little longer.

Now that the car quit bouncing—they were on paved road again—Sterling let his head rest against the trunk's floor. The ringing in his ears started to subside, but it felt like a migraine was taking its place. A wave of nausea ran over him.

Sterling had survived a dangerous life as the Satan's Dawgs' bookkeeper. The danger didn't lessen after his entry into the Witness Protection Program. Sterling's old club as well as factions of the American mob wanted him dead which made his current predicament feel incredibly embarrassing.

He escaped repeated run-ins with professional killers only to be nabbed by members of the Maple Leaf Mafia. His nausea worsened as the humiliation of getting caught by Canadian gangsters wormed its way into his brain.

Sterling frowned in the darkness of the trunk. The Maple Leafs didn't behave how he imagined Canadians were supposed to act. His position in the trunk proved that.

Which meant what exactly?

Maybe a kaleidoscope of people lived in Canada. If that was true, the country had all types like the United States. Polite citizens living alongside rude neighbors. Nice folks dealing with awful people. Greedy politicians and misunderstood criminals always looking for an advantage.

Was Canada like the United States, only with more snow and an affinity for hockey? If that was true, Sterling had unfairly judged an entire country. It was exactly how citizens used to judge him because of his long hair and riding leathers he wore with the club.

Sterling groaned. The concussion was affecting his thinking. He needed to focus.

Canada, he reminded himself, was a mirror of Minnesota—cold, snowy, and overly polite. Nothing was going to change those facts which meant Sterling wasn't wrong about his opinions. He felt better, knowing the concussion wouldn't cloud his thoughts for long.

The car turned again, forcing Sterling to slide toward his feet. When the Lexus straightened, he pushed himself back into the middle of the trunk.

Sterling's fingers traveled about the darkness, looking for an emergency release. Every new car had one. Their existence was mandated by law. He didn't find the quick pull, so he searched again, his fingers fumbling over every surface. Eventually, he gave up.

The mobsters had obviously removed the emergency release. For criminal kidnappers, it was a smart move. Sterling's former self, the bookkeeper, would have done the same thing. The thought didn't make him happy.

He lay his head back on the trunk's floor and stopped worrying. His opportunity for escape would come soon. He'd just have to be ready for it.

The cold in his bones deepened as his wet clothing stuck to him. No heat from the interior made it to the trunk. Sterling shivered as his body struggled to generate warmth.

Sterling closed his eyes even though he knew he shouldn't. If he indeed had a concussion, he shouldn't sleep. However, the darkness felt oddly comforting given the cramped confines he found himself in.

As the Lexus weaved through Wandering Springs—he assumed they were still in the small town—Sterling's thoughts bounced from his grandmother to Daphne Winterbourne. Just as he was about to worry about never seeing either of them again, Sterling's thoughts jumped once more.

His life had changed dramatically since entering the Witness Protection Program. Living under various aliases had allowed him to see a different side of life, something better than living in the brotherhood of the Satan's Dawgs. Before he could spend too much time ruminating on that, Sterling's thoughts switched to his cat.

If something happened to Sterling, Travis probably wouldn't even care if Sterling was no longer around so long as someone fed him in a timely manner. When was the last time Sterling fed the little guy? Should he change his brand of food?

Sterling realized his thoughts were erratic and tried to focus on the reason why. Were they a symptom of his concussion or simply a result of being tired? Whatever the cause, Sterling struggled to remain in the moment. He needed to act, even in the small confines of the trunk, to help give his brain something tangible to hold onto.

He extended his legs slightly, pressing his feet into the side of the car. This caused his body to contort further, smashing his shoulder into the opposite side. The resulting pain overwhelmed his tiredness and his thoughts became more focused on his immediate pain.

Sterling shifted his weight so his arm could slide behind him and reach into his back pocket. It was empty. The Maple Leafs had taken his cell phone. He shifted once more so he could check the other pocket. The mobsters had also removed his wallet.

The car turned right, and the bumping started again. Sterling tried to maintain his uncomfortable position, but the Lexus hit a large pothole and dislodged him. He was tossed again before the sedan abruptly stopped. Sterling's left arm was pinned underneath him, and his right was stuck behind his back.

Car doors opened, and footsteps hurried outside. The lid popped and rain fell into the small confines of the trunk.

Rhys, Lark, and Theo stood in the downpour. Confusion etched their faces. Lark and Theo held their guns in front of them. Sterling tried to look beyond them to figure out where they might be, but all he could tell for certain was they were in another alley somewhere. The potholes had already told him that.

The boss tossed Sterling's wallet into the trunk, hitting him in the chest. He asked, "Care to explain this?"

"It was a present." Sterling shifted his weight so he could pick up the wallet.

"Cute," Theo said.

Lark eyed the boss. "Let's just shoot him."

"Not 'til we get some answers."

Theo grunted. "I get the feeling this guy ain't gonna talk."

Now, Rhys waggled Sterling's flip phone. "What about this? Gonna tell me it's a present, too?"

"No," Sterling said. "That I found."

"Why aren't there any numbers in it?"

"I don't know anyone."

Rhys cocked his head. "You called one number."

"Butt dial."

"It's a flip phone."

Sterling pushed himself onto his elbow but decided there was no easy way for him to hop out of the trunk. Once he made it out, he'd have to immediately fight the mobsters, two of which were armed. To make matters worse, his actions and thoughts would be hampered by his twisted ankle and the lingering effects of a possible concussion.

The boss sucked air through his teeth. "You aren't real, Sterling Carter. Are you?"

"The ringing in my head says otherwise."

"This guy," Lark muttered. "Always with the smart mouth." She pointed her gun at Sterling. "I'll take care of that ringing for you."

Rain splashed against the boss's face, but he didn't seem concerned by it. "We called you in."

That phrase carried different meanings. An employer who said it was likely to issue some discipline to an underperforming employee. The cops said it whenever one of them requested a dispatcher run an arrestee's name through the criminal database. The phrase coming from the Maple Leaf boss likely meant he alerted his superior that they had a U.S. citizen in their trunk.

"You know what they said?" Rhys asked.

"I'm hoping it was let him go."

Lark lifted her gun higher. "One more smart comment and I'll shoot you in the face."

Theo shrugged, still holding his gun in front of his waist. "He ain't gonna talk."

"They found nothing," the boss said. "Our connections in law enforcement found bupkis on you. Boring, old Sterling Carter. No criminal history. Last of the good guys."

"What can I say?" Sterling asked. "That's how my grandmother raised me."

"I'll bet."

"Please," Lark said, "I'll say it was an

accident. Bang. Oops."

Theo nodded. "I'm with her. Let's do him and get out of the rain."

Rhys lifted his hand, quieting them. He said to Sterling. "Why'd you attack my people?"

"They kept asking stupid questions."

"All right, tough guy. Have it your way." Rhys waved Lark and Theo forward. "Shoot him."

"Wait," Sterling said, lifting his free hand into the air. "Just wait."

Rhys stepped forward, motioning for Lark and Theo to lower their guns. "Last chance," he said. "The truth."

"I work at the cupcakery."

Lark sneered. "The guy is begging to be shot."

The boss shook his head. "Easy, now."

"How about one in the leg?" Theo suggested. He pointed his gun at Sterling's knee. "To let him know how serious we are."

"He's talking," Rhys said. His eyes narrowed as he spoke to Sterling. "As long as he keeps it up, there's no need to shoot him."

Sterling pushed higher up on his elbow. "When you asked about Norma Jean—"

"Who?" the boss interrupted.

"The owner of the cupcake store." Sterling's gaze darted to Lark and Theo. "When you asked about her, I got worried."

"What did you have to worry about?" Rhys asked. His gaze cut to Lark, and he pushed the barrel of her gun down. He smiled, even as the rain continued to pelt his face. "We don't want to hurt her. We just want to ask some questions.

Nice like."

"What kind of questions?" Sterling asked, even though he knew the answer.

"That's our business," the boss said. "Why didn't you tell us where she lives?"

Sterling brought his legs up and tried to set his feet on the floor of the trunk. If he jumped now, he'd go out at an angle. There was no way for him to easily scramble free. He needed the Maple Leafs to invite him out of the trunk. He relaxed slightly.

"I didn't know her address when you asked," Sterling said.

Lark lifted her chin in Sterling's direction. "He's stalling."

The boss set his hand on her shoulder. To Sterling, he said, "But then you found out where she lives. Am I right?"

"I did."

Rhys motioned toward Sterling. "All this unpleasantness could have been avoided if you cooperated from the beginning. Where's she live?"

"I don't know the address."

"This guy," Lark blurted and raised her gun.

"He talks in circles," Theo said, also lifting his gun.

"I know where she lives," Sterling said, "but I don't know the address. I'll have to show you."

Rhys frowned. "Get him out."

***

Sterling sat in the back seat with his hands tucked into his pockets and a seatbelt around his waist and over his arms. The Maple Leafs insisted he sit that way before they even entered the car. He was the only one wearing a seatbelt.

Theo clutched his gun, his eyes alert, as he watched Sterling from the neighboring seat. The boss had moved to the passenger seat while Lark continued to pilot the car.

Rhys turned to eye Sterling. "Ever meet Pearl MacKenzie?"

"Canadian Pearl?" Sterling asked.

"How many Pearls live in this town?"

Sterling shrugged.

"Seen her lately?"

"She was in yesterday." Sterling didn't see harm in telling the truth about Pearl's visit to Frosty Petal. "For a batch of cupcakes."

"Sounds like her," Rhys said. "What about this morning? Seen her?"

"No," Sterling lied. "That's the person you're looking for?"

"It is."

"You tracked her here?" Sterling asked. "To Wandering Springs?"

Rhys grinned. "Look at you, trying to get us to reveal our secrets."

"Guy thinks he's smarter than us." Theo sniggered.

Lark's cell phone rang, and she answered it. "Uh-huh. Yeah. Got it. What? I'll ask." She hung up, then eyed her boss. "Declan got the car started."

"What're they doing now?" Rhys asked.

"Asking about breakfast."

"Breakfast?"

"I could go for a coffee," Theo said.

"Me too," Lark added, "if we're being honest."

Theo jerked his head. "What about that French bakery? Should be open soon."

Rhys sighed. "After we find Pearl, we'll get a coffee." He asked over his shoulder. "Where to, tough guy?"

Sterling lifted his chin. "Once you're out of the alley, hang a left."

The car rocked forward and immediately hit its first pothole. Theo's gun bounced up and down.

"Mind taking your finger off the trigger?" Sterling asked.

"Relax, princess," Theo said with a confident smirk, "Nothing's gonna happen—"

The car bounced over another pothole and the gun rocked in Theo's hand. Sterling flinched as the weapon fired. Lark slammed on the brakes which caused Theo to slide off his seat and careen into the back of the boss. The gun fired a second time.

Each mobster spewed a string of expletives, but the boss's filthy rant overpowered the others. He'd slipped out of his seat from the combination of the sudden stop and Theo's force. Rhys pushed himself up from the floorboard and spun around, his face purple with anger.

Lark slammed the transmission into Park

and glared over her shoulder.

Theo sheepishly straightened himself and flopped back in his seat. He held the gun with both hands like a child cradles a wounded bird.

Sterling remained seated with his hands in his pockets and the belt secured over his torso. Perhaps in another situation he would have moved quicker and taken advantage of the confusion. However, the gunshots surprised him, and the abrupt stop threw him into the seatbelt. He still felt fuzzy from his earlier fall. The ringing in his ears worsened from the proximity of two gunshots.

"You coulda killed me!" Rhys barked.

Theo stared at the gun, obviously ashamed to look up. "It was an accident."

"An accident?" the boss stammered. "Tough guy told you to take your finger off the trigger."

Water dripped into the car. Everyone's gaze drifted to a bullet hole in the roof of the Lexus.

"You shot the car," Lark said with mild amusement.

The boss watched rainwater drip onto the back seat for a moment before turning his attention to Sterling. Something caught his eye, and his attention went to the window next to Sterling's shoulder.

Theo leaned forward so he could see the window better. He groaned.

"What is it?" Lark asked as she flopped left and right. "What do you see?"

The second bullet had flown through the rear passenger window, leaving a perfectly clean hole without fracturing the glass.

"Great. Just great." The boss angrily waved at the window. "How do we explain that at the border?"

"It was an accident," Theo repeated.

"You're an accident." The boss snapped his fingers and opened his hand. "Gimme the gun."

"I'm supposed to watch him." Theo's eyes darted between Sterling and the boss.

"That's right, you are." He snapped his fingers again. "Now you're gonna do it without the piece."

Theo sighed and bobbled his head before setting the gun in the boss's hand.

"If he gives you any trouble—" The boss lifted his chin in Sterling's direction. "—slug him."

"Oh, I can do that." Theo raised his fist.

"Careful not to punch a hole in the car," Lark said.

Before Theo could protest, the Lexus lurched forward.

***

"This is taking too long," Rhys grumbled. He turned in his seat and let the gun hang casually from his hand. "This better not be a wild goose chase."

"I'm lost," Sterling lied. He moved his jaw, hoping to quiet the ringing in his ears.

The water trickling in from the bullet hole picked up steam. The droplets fell onto the seat between Sterling and Theo. The wipers flicked faster over the windshield.

"Lost? In this tiny burg?" The boss smirked. "You're spinning us around in circles is what you're doing." He pointed the gun at Sterling. "We better arrive in two minutes, or I'll shoot you myself."

Sterling wanted to waste time. The more he spent with the Maple Leafs, the less time they were focusing on Pearl or Norma Jean. However, there was a limit to how long something like that could drag on, especially in a small town like Wandering Springs.

His head felt slightly clearer now, but the ringing in his ears remained. Sterling had been hit hard before and knew the brain fog wouldn't completely go away for a couple of days. It was something he could work through.

Even if the sludge in his head cleared completely, Sterling still had a problem. A seatbelt secured him to the back seat, pinning his hands in his pockets. It wasn't the toughest problem to solve. Sterling could pull his hands free before undoing the buckle to free himself. The issue was time. One of the Maple Leafs, if not all, would notice his sudden movement and they'd act.

"It's up ahead," Sterling said. "On the right."

Rhys spun in his seat. "Which house?"

"The yellow one."

Sterling wasn't worried about Norma Jean being home since she was hiding at Chateau Sweets. He was certain Pearl wouldn't go to Norma Jean's since she knew the Maple Leafs were still looking for her. Sterling also didn't want to give a different house and send the mobsters after innocent bystanders. It was best to keep this problem contained.

"Pull over," the boss instructed.

Lark jerked the wheel and directed the Lexus to a spot along the curb. She slipped the car into Park.

"We're gonna check this out," the boss said over his shoulder. "You better not be lying."

Sterling didn't defend himself.

Theo popped open his door and started to step out.

"Not you." Rhys turned in his seat to see Theo better. "You stay here with him."

"In that case." Theo yanked the door closed. "I need my gun."

"To shoot the car again?" Lark asked.

"Zip it," Rhys said. He handed the gun to Theo, then cut his gaze to Sterling. "You do anything stupid, he's gonna shoot you."

"I understand."

The boss's lips twisted as he studied Sterling. "You're pretty calm for a guy experiencing the worst day of his life."

"I guess I'm in shock," Sterling said flatly.

"Shock?" the boss asked.

"Probably." He shrugged with his hands still stuck in his pockets and pinned by the seatbelt.

Lark's eyes drifted to the rearview mirror. "Something ain't right with this one, eh?"

"He gives you trouble," the boss said to Theo, "any problems at all, waste him."

"You got it." Theo seemed pleased with the thought.

Rhys spun in his seat, swung open the door, and exited the car. Lark followed him closely as they walked up the sidewalk to Norma Jean's house.

Sterling pretended to watch the two outside the car, but his mind was on the man sitting next to him. Theo's attention, however, was completely on Sterling. He had yet to look back in the direction of his comrades.

Rain fell through the hole in the ceiling as the storm raged outside. The patter of droplets on the leather seat developed a steady rhythm now that the car had stopped.

"Really coming down," Sterling muttered. "Does it rain like this in Canada?"

"What do you take me for—a weatherman?"

Sterling watched Rhys and Lark as they approached Norma Jean's house. He tried to make it seem like the most interesting scene he'd ever watched. Theo didn't bite and continued to study Sterling.

"Where you from?" Sterling asked.

"None of your business."

"Just being friendly."

"I don't need a friend." Theo waved the gun. "Shut your mouth before I shut it for you."

Sterling leaned forward slightly, trying to show how interested he was in what was occurring on the front stoop of Norma Jean's house. Rhys knocked as Lark kept watch for anyone moving in the neighborhood.

"Looks like no one's home," Sterling said.

"Too bad for you." Theo absently waved the gun barrel. It pointed at Sterling, moved away, only to return.

Rhys said something to Lark, and she hopped down the stairs. Lark moved toward the side of Norma Jean's house. Theo still hadn't looked in their direction.

Sterling frowned. "They're waving for you," he lied.

Theo started to turn his head but suddenly paused. Suspicion flooded his eyes. "Don't try anything funny."

"I'm not the one they're asking for."

Theo sniffed dismissively and looked over his shoulder. He squinted to see through the rain and darkness. "Who waved?"

"The boss," Sterling said. He slipped his hands from his pockets. "What's his face?" Sterling coughed once as he unclicked the seatbelt. He caught it before it could slide back and make any noise.

Theo leaned closer to the window. "I don't see—"

Sterling slammed Theo's face into the glass and the gun fired into the floorboard. The high-pitched ringing intensified in Sterling's ears. He grabbed Theo's head and smashed it once more into the window. The enforcer slumped in his seat.

Outside, Rhys and Lark turned toward the Lexus, momentarily confused at what they'd heard.

Sterling desperately searched for the gun but couldn't find it. He spun, shoved open the door, and jumped into the rain. His injured ankle squealed at the sudden weight on it.

"Get him!" Rhys yelled.

Sterling hurriedly limped across the street. He cut through the yard of a blue rancher and approached a tall wooden fence. He pulled on the gate, but it was locked. Sterling hopped on the fence and pulled himself up, swinging his legs over the top of his head. He came down on a concrete path, but his bad ankle gave way, sending him sprawling into the wet lawn.

Lark jumped on the fence. She threw her gun hand over the top to support herself. "Stop," she said. Her feet kicked at the fence.

Sterling rolled away, then righted himself.

"I'll shoot," she groaned at him while pulling herself further over the fence.

If she let go now to aim the gun, she'd likely slip off the fence. Sterling backpedaled twice, wobbling because of the bad ankle. He turned and quickly limped for the far fence. He had to get to it before Lark entered the backyard.

Sterling went as fast as he could. His head remained foggy and the ringing in his ears was constant. With each step, the grass underfoot felt squishy, and Sterling worried about falling. He made it to the back gate and yanked it open.

A shot fired, its crack pierced the steady rhythm of the rain. A chunk of fence exploded near Sterling's hand. He stumbled through the gate and belly flopped into the alley. His breath escaped his lungs in one sudden exhale, and he sucked for air.

Sterling couldn't lay there. He needed to move even if he couldn't breathe. Lark would arrive at the back fence soon. If she found him on his stomach, it'd be like shooting fish in a barrel.

He pushed himself to his hands and knees. The pain in his chest was excruciating. He gasped for air and his legs churned against the protests of his ankle, propelling him forward.

Sterling finally righted himself into a crouching, limping run and headed for the end of the alley.

No more shots followed.

Chapter 12

Sterling's hobbling worsened the farther he went. He'd gone two blocks when he stopped to hide in the shadow of a sagging garage. He struggled to catch his breath and bent at the knees. Sterling didn't run for exercise, but this short distance shouldn't have caused him such trouble. He greedily sucked in air. Perhaps the accumulation of his injuries and the cold caused the shortness of breath.

The storm continued to rage, and rain ran off the sagging garage roof cascading to the alley below. Sterling hunched under an eave. It was little protection since he was already soaked.

As the tightness in Sterling's chest eased, frustration grew in the pit of his stomach.

Canadians were supposed to be nice. Considering the morning's events, it was a stupid belief. Yet that's how Sterling always thought of people from the Great White North. In fact, the Satan's Dawgs hated the entire country because of their affable nature. Yet, the Maple Leafs weren't mellow or kind. They were dangerous. Based upon the situation he found himself in this morning, Sterling put them on par with his old club and the American mob.

It seemed Sterling might've misjudged an entire country. It's something a better man certainly wouldn't do. To make matters worse, if he admitted he misjudged Canada, then he probably should consider the possibility he did the same to Minnesota. This caused the frustration in his gut to sour.

"No," he muttered to himself. Changing his opinion on the Gopher State was taking this pursuit of improvement one step too far.

A better man might value the nutritional benefit of vegetables, but Sterling wasn't going to start eating broccoli now. Minnesota was America's broccoli, and that's all there was to it.

Breathing easier now, Sterling straightened and moved to the edge of the shadow, still underneath the overhang. He peered down the alley in both directions. No one moved, and no headlights crept past the alley openings.

The sky was brightening. Not because the storm was easing, but it was clear the sun was trying to break through the eastern horizon. It wouldn't be long before the nearest border crossing opened. Either the Maple Leafs would slip back into their country or reinforcements would arrive.

Sterling preferred the former, but was pretty sure the latter would happen.

The sun's arrival meant the citizens were also awaking. Some might have heard Lark's gunshot. Perhaps someone was awoken by the BMW's collision with the tree. Would law enforcement arrive shortly to check on the strange occurrences happening in Wandering Springs? If so, would they be cops Sterling could trust?

He couldn't worry about that now. Instead, Sterling needed to ensure Norma Jean and Pearl were okay, then formulate a plan to stay safe until either the marshals or the Mounties arrived.

Sterling stepped out from the shadows and limped toward Chateau Sweets.

***

Sterling knocked on the back door of the French bakery. He continued to scan left and right, hoping the Maple Leafs didn't pull into the alley now. If one of the Canadian mobsters found him here, it could be disastrous for everyone.

"Who is it?" Marion Bardot called from inside.

"Sterling Carter."

The latch noisily slid back, and the door barely cracked open. Marion's eye appeared and she quickly appraised Sterling. Satisfied he was indeed who he said he was, she shuffled backward and pulled open the door with her. "Get in here before you catch your death."

Sterling stepped inside and closed the door behind him. He slid the latch into place.

"Oh my," Marion said. "Don't move. You're all muddy. What happened?"

"Trouble." Sterling faced her. "Did Pearl make it?"

"I'm here," Pearl MacKenzie said from around the corner. She and Norma Jean appeared with small towels draped over their shoulders. Both had cups of coffee, but Pearl also held a half-eaten croissant. Given the situation, they seemed rather relaxed.

The aroma of baking pastries filled the small kitchen, and the heat from the various ovens warmed Sterling.

Norma Jean's brow furrowed "You look a fright, Silver."

"I've had better mornings."

"Haven't we all?" Pearl said as she stuffed the final bite of croissant into her mouth. "Is it safe out there?"

"Not even a little." Sterling eyed Marion. "Mind if I use your phone?"

Norma Jean pulled the towel from her shoulders and handed it to him. "Time we call the cops?"

Pearl swallowed and saluted him with her mug. "The Mounties know I'm here. My handler said they're working with your marshals to get me to safety. Shouldn't be long now."

Sterling dried his hair with the small towel. "The phone?" he asked again.

Marion grimaced as she considered Sterling's condition. "Try not to touch anything else." She motioned toward a wireless phone hanging on a wall.

Sterling limped through the kitchen, careful not to slip on the tile floor. Falling now would only frustrate him further. He grabbed the phone and dialed the emergency number he'd memorized.

The call was answered on the first ring.

"Krumland," the marshal said.

"It's me." Sterling moved farther away from the women but stayed out of sight of the front windows.

"What number are you calling from?"

"Chateau Sweets."

"A candy store?"

"Bakery."

Krumland grunted. "You brought another civilian into this mess?"

"Had no choice."

"You have some major trouble going on there."

"That's what I told you." Sterling flipped the wet towel over his shoulder.

"You don't understand," Krumland said. "One of the thugs called me, wanting to know who I was."

"What'd you tell him?"

"I said he got a wrong number." Krumland scoffed. "What do you think I told him?"

"I don't know."

"He called from your number, Beau. How'd that happen?"

"I had a run in with them. They took my phone."

"What did you tell them?"

"Nothing."

Krumland sighed. "So your cover might be intact?"

"I doubt it. They've got my wallet."

"How'd they get that?"

"Same way they got the phone."

"Maybe they won't dig deeper into you," Krumland said. There was no optimism in the statement. "Probably depends on how much of a thorn you've been in their sides."

Marion handed another pastry to a grateful Pearl while Norma Jean watched their interaction with disapproval.

Sterling asked, "What'd he say?"

"Who?"

"The guy who called from my phone."

"He didn't say much," Krumland said. "When I refused to tell him who I was and how I knew you, he hung up."

"That'd be Rhys, the boss."

"Rhys," Krumland said. "Got a last name?"

"We didn't exactly exchange business cards."

"No need to be smart about it."

Sterling asked, "How far off is our help?"

"Going to be a bit."

"Of course it is."

"Agents from Seattle are headed your way, but several rivers have overflowed and caused flooding throughout multiple counties. Traffic is jammed up everywhere. All of Whatcom County's emergency services are dedicated to the flooding as are a bunch of smaller agencies."

"When something can go wrong..." Sterling muttered.

"Certainly seems that way," Krumland said. "Take heart, though. We've contacted other law enforcement for help. Deputies from Okanogan County are responding. Probably another hour. They're running code to get there. You going to stay at the bakery?"

Sterling looked toward Norma Jean and Pearl. "We're going to move."

"Why's that?"

"The Maple Leafs were talking about stopping here for breakfast. With how bad their morning's been, I could see them taking a break to regroup."

"You giving them a rough time?" Krumland asked.

"Trying to keep them busy. What about the Mounties? Are they sending someone down for Pearl?"

"They are," Krumland said. "They're driving your way now."

"The nearest border crossing is still closed."

"Not for them."

"Right," Sterling said. "Not for them."

"When you get where you're going, call me and let me know. I'll pass it on to them."

Sterling thought Pearl was already in contact with her handlers, but Sterling said, "Will do."

"And Beau?"

"Yeah?"

"Take care of yourself." Krumland ended the call.

Sterling stared at the phone, surprised at the lawman's concern. He hung up the device and turned to Pearl. "We've got to find another place."

"We can't stay here?"

"The Maple Leafs are hungry, and they talked about coming here for breakfast."

Norma Jean appeared offended. "Why wouldn't they come by the Frosty Petal for a muffin? Our muffins are good." She looked at Pearl. "You think they're good, right?"

Pearl shrugged. "They're fine."

"Fine?" Norma Jean stiffened. "I thought you liked our muffins."

"I'd rather have a croissant," Pearl said sheepishly. "No offense."

"None taken." Marion grinned. "I completely understand."

Norma Jean huffed. "Well, I'm offended."

"We're getting off topic," Sterling said.

"Let's be honest," Marion said. "Muffins are breakfast cupcakes."

"What's wrong with that?" Norma Jean's face reddened. "Cupcakes are special."

"Eh." Marion smirked. "How special can they be if anyone can make them from a box?"

"Ladies," Sterling said, but no one paid him any attention.

"I never—" Norma Jean stammered. "Never." Her gaze drifted to Pearl. "And you!"

"What'd I do?"

"You didn't defend my cupcakes."

Pearl lightly touched her chest. "I *love* your cupcakes."

"Just not my muffins." Norma Jean crossed her arms. "Well, help yourself. What do I care? Have another croissant or one of those stupid cinnamon rolls."

"*Pain aux raisin*," Marion corrected.

Norma Jean blew a raspberry.

Sterling stepped forward. "Ladies, we need to focus. The Maple Leafs said they were coming here when Marion opens."

The women briefly eyed Sterling then smiled apologetically at each other.

"This argument can wait," Norma Jean said.

Marion nodded once. "I agree."

"All this talk about pastries is making me hungry," Pearl said. "Mind if I have one of those *pain aux raisins*?"

Sterling held up his hands, hoping to stop any further talk about French delicacies. "We need to find somewhere else to go."

"How about your place?" Norma Jean asked.

He shook his head. "They have my wallet."

"Which has your address." She nodded. "Yeah, that makes sense."

"Can we call one of your friends?" Pearl asked Norma Jean.

Sterling interrupted. "We don't want to bring anyone else into this if we can help it." His eyes cut to Marion. "I'm already sorry we brought you into it."

She waved his apology away. "This has been the most fun I've had since my husband died."

Everyone stared at her.

Marion frowned. "That sounded bad."

"A little," Norma Jean agreed.

"What I meant to say is this morning has been the most fun I've had in years."

Norma Jean and Pearl eyed her curiously.

"We could take my car," Marion said quickly, "and leave the city."

"What do you say, Silver?" Norma Jean asked. "Let's hit the road."

He didn't like the idea of being on the road with the three women in a bright red Subaru. It felt too exposed if the Maple Leafs somehow caught up to them. Also, it would make coordinating with Marshal Krumland harder if Sterling had to continually update his location.

Still, there was something to be said for making it harder on the Canadian mob. If the four of them could leave town without the mob knowing, they'd be home free. However, if the Maple Leafs caught them, they'd be stuck in the open.

If he only had to worry about himself, Sterling would have risked it, especially if he had a gun. Maybe even if he didn't, like now, he'd chance it. Yet he had the lives of three others to consider.

"The best option," Sterling said, "is for us to find another place to hide." His gaze bounced between Norma Jean and Marion. "Any suggestions?"

"My house?" the Chateau Sweets owner said.

"How far?" Sterling asked.

"Ten blocks."

"The edge of town," Norma Jean said. She pointed at the business's front window. "Due south."

Sterling gritted his teeth. He didn't want to move that far, especially with the sun coming up. Four people hurrying through a city would be hard to miss, especially for ten blocks.

"Something closer," he said.

"We can go back to Norma Jean's," Pearl suggested.

"The Maple Leafs know where you live now."

"They do?" She appeared confused. "How'd they find my address?"

Sterling dismissively waved his hand. "Let's not focus on that now. Other ideas?"

Norma Jean shook her head. "The only ideas I have will bring others into our problem."

Sterling ran his fingers through his wet hair, then looked toward the front window. His gaze drifted along the businesses across the street. That's when he remembered a conversation from yesterday. He said, "I have an idea."

Chapter 13

Sterling hunched his shoulders as protection from the pouring rain. He left via the back door after making sure no Canadian mobsters were lying in wait. He hobbled through the alley as quickly as he could, keeping alert. He didn't like moving through town again, but if his idea worked, they'd all have a safe place to hide until the authorities arrived.

Droplets pelted the pothole puddles in the alley. The rain hid the sound of his footsteps. Sterling left the safety of the shadows, crossed the street, and entered another alley.

His limp was more pronounced now, but he mostly ignored the pain. The fog in his head had cleared and the ringing in his ears was almost gone.

Sterling had a mission now—reach Cozy Corner, the only bookstore in Wandering Springs. Yesterday, Eleanor Spradlin said she was leaving to visit her sister in Portland after closing the store. It was a perfect place to hide if he could get in.

When he cleared the next block, he darted as fast as a man with a bum ankle could toward Main Street. He searched for the white Lexus or the black BMW. Not seeing either, Sterling hurried across Main Street and past the bookstore's front door. He continued around the building and into the alley.

Sterling hoped for two possibilities—that Cozy Corner didn't have great locks and there wasn't a security system. Small town bookstores weren't likely to be a prime target for crime, but he didn't bring Norma Jean or Pearl with him on the chance he was wrong. If an alarm blared at this time of morning, it would certainly attract attention. Better to be alone in case he needed to dart into the nearby neighborhood.

He entered the alley and passed the rear of Frosty Petal. He continued to Cozy Corner, made sure he was alone, then approached the bookstore's back door. Sterling wasn't a master at picking locks. A couple of other guys in the Satan's Dawgs were proficient burglars, but he never learned the skill. His talents centered around violence.

Sterling had broken into buildings before, of course, but always with brute force. This morning would be no different. He thought about kicking the door, but he'd either have to use his bad ankle as support, or he'd use the foot it was attached to as a battering ram. Sterling dismissed both options.

He banged his shoulder into the door and the lock gave way. Sterling stepped inside and closed the door behind him. He listened for a moment, hoping not to hear the tell-tale beep of an alarm system. Not all of them had audible alerts. Some businesses had silent alarms wherein they hoped to catch an intruder by not revealing a control panel's location. Those systems always waited a few seconds before calling the police.

Sterling hoped Eleanor Spradlin hadn't gone to that extreme. If anything, he imagined Cozy Corner would have a simple alarm—one that would blare without alerting the cops if someone failed to enter the proper code.

The rain continued to fall outside, and it made hearing any beeps difficult. Sterling moved deeper into the darkened bookstore and the noise of the late-winter weather faded. The only brightness in the store came from the ambient glow of the streetlights lining Main Street.

When Sterling wore the Satan's Dawgs leathers, he never felt bad for illegally entering a home or business. Breaking the law was as common as eating breakfast. Now, however, he felt a strange sensation. Not quite guilt, but something akin to it.

Shame, perhaps? He couldn't put his finger on it.

During business hours, Cozy Corner was a magical place. It had an ability to whisk him away from his troubles. He shouldn't be there now, standing by himself in the dark.

Sterling never read a book outside of high school. Those he did while in school were assigned by a teacher, and he never got any enjoyment out of them. Books had helped change his life over the past months. They alone wouldn't make him a better man, but reading certainly helped him feel smarter and happier.

He couldn't linger on the feeling of shame for long. Sterling needed to protect Norma Jean and Pearl, and that's why he broke into the bookstore.

Sterling unlocked the front door and stepped underneath the striped awning. Water rolled off the angled canvas, protecting Sterling from the storm. He checked to make sure Main Street was still clear before pulling the door closed behind him. Sterling hobbled across the street back to Chateau Sweets.

***

Pearl MacKenzie looked up, embarrassed, as Sterling entered the kitchen through the rear door. She held a cup of coffee in her left hand and another half-eaten croissant in her right. "I'm gut-foundered," she said, before nibbling on the pastry.

Norma Jean, sensing Sterling's confusion, interpreted. "She's starving. I don't know how since that's her fourth pastry."

"We've got to go," he said.

Pearl's gaze frantically bounced between the croissant and coffee. "But I'm not done," she said.

"Make it fast." Sterling turned his attention to Marion who removed a tray of pastries from an oven. "You should come, too."

"They're not after me," she said. Marion set the tray down, then casually waved her oven mitt over it. "I'll be fine."

Norma Jean clucked. "She wants a day to steal all my customers."

Marion's jaw dropped. "That's not it."

"Sure it is." Norma Jean's face reddened. "Admit it."

"How can you say that?" Marion motioned toward Pearl. "I'm letting you and your friend hide here—"

"Which is lulling me into thinking we could be friends again after all these years."

"Fine," Marian said. She tossed the oven mitt aside. "If going along is what it will take for us to bury the hatchet, so be it."

Norma Jean's face pinched before she contemptuously waved. "I don't care what you do."

"One at a time," Sterling said. "Who's first?"

Once again, Pearl lifted her coffee and half-eaten pastry.

"Guess it's me," Norma Jean said. She stepped forward. "Where are we going?"

"The bookstore."

"Eleanor's?"

Sterling nodded. "She's gone for a couple days. It's a perfect place to hide."

He opened the back door, inspected the alley, then waved for Norma Jean to follow. The two hurried through the alley. With his limp slowing him down, Norma Jean actually led the way.

She glanced over her shoulder. "Hurry up, Silver."

They slowed at each street they came to

before scampering into the shadows of the next alley. When the two arrived at the businesses across the street from the bookstore, Sterling and Norma Jean crept toward the sidewalk.

"Since we're here," Norma Jean said, "how about I hide at the Petal? It's not too late for me to get a few batches started."

"If the Maple Leafs see a light on in the bakery, they'll come for you."

"I could work in the dark."

"Pearl," Sterling said.

She frowned. "Whatever."

He scanned Main Street. "The front door's unlocked," Sterling said.

"I'm going by myself?"

"I've got to get the others."

"In that case, wish me luck."

She scurried across the street. It was the fastest Sterling had ever seen her move. When she made it to Cozy Corner, Norma Jean stepped inside without hesitation.

Sterling waved goodbye then slipped into the alley shadows. He hobbled back to Chateau Sweets, yanked open the door, and said, "Your turn."

"Almost ready," Pearl said, holding up a finger asking Sterling to wait.

Marion handed her a small bag. "Here you go."

"Thank you," she said with a smile. Pearl turned to Sterling. "Ready now."

He eyed her quizzically.

"Travel snacks," she said while stepping by

him.

They hurried through the alley, following the same route Sterling had taken twice before. He thought about altering the course but diverting now seemed additionally reckless. Every moment felt tortuous, as if he and Pearl would be discovered by the Maple Leafs at any second.

When they made it to businesses across from Cozy Corner, Sterling motioned for Pearl to step forward. "Go to the bookstore," he said. "Norma Jean's waiting for you."

Before letting her go, Sterling made sure nothing moved on Main Street. He patted Pearl's shoulder. "Now."

She trotted across the road, not as fast as Norma Jean, but much quicker than Sterling thought possible. The door to Cozy Corner opened just as Pearl arrived. When she stepped in, Norma Jean waved at Sterling, then pulled the door closed.

He lingered for a moment. Marion said she wanted to stay in her shop. Sterling could run across Main Street now and hide in the bookstore until help arrived.

However, if the Maple Leafs did show up at the French bakery and hassled Marion for any reason, Sterling would feel terrible he didn't try to convince her to come at least once more.

He backed away from Main Street while limping to Chateau Sweets.

***

Sterling stepped through the back door of the French bakery. He didn't move any further into the store since his clothing was dripping water onto the shoe mat. The kitchen's warmth enveloped him like a blanket.

"Ready?" he asked.

Marion didn't look up as she scooped coffee grounds into a large filter. "I'm staying. It's almost six." As if to prove Marion's point, she motioned toward the clock on the wall.

He wiped his feet twice before stepping forward. It was a futile action because water still dripped from his clothing. "If you open the doors, they'll show up."

"I know, but so will my other customers." Marion's eyes dipped to the floor. "You're making a mess."

Sterling ignored her concerns about slippery tiles. "Why do you want your regulars coming in?"

"So we can let them know what's going on."

"It'll bring them harm."

Marion rolled her eyes. "That's not how the truth works. Once it gets into the light, everyone will be safe. Cedric always stood for what was right. I'm going to do that, too."

It was a cute thought, but Sterling knew better. The truth often brought deadly consequences. As far as he was concerned, ignorance remained the best policy when it came to citizens. Keep them in the dark as long as possible.

"Besides," Marion said, "the police will be

here soon and this whole situation will be resolved."

"If it isn't?" Sterling asked, once again moving closer.

Marion set the coffee machine's brewing cycle. "For someone working with cupcakes, you sure are a pessimist."

"I'm a realist."

"If you're going to drip water everywhere, the least you could do is clean it up." Marion motioned toward the mop and bucket in the corner.

Before Sterling could protest, someone knocked on the front door.

Marion eyed Sterling. "Here we go, first customer of the day."

"Hold on," he said.

He moved toward the wall separating the lobby from the kitchen and leaned around the corner, taking care not to expose much of himself. Standing near the front window were Lark and Rhys. Theo banged again on the door.

"It's them," Sterling whispered as he moved out of sight. "The Maple Leafs."

Marion shrugged. "I'm not afraid."

"You should be."

"They want something to eat. I'll help them, and they'll be on their way. Maybe they'll even be nicer after they taste something delicious. You've never witnessed the healing power of French pastries."

Sterling opened his mouth to argue, but Marion slipped by him. He moved so he could watch the interaction in the lobby. If anything happened, Sterling would rush to Marion's aid. He wasn't sure why something like that would occur, but he'd be ready, nonetheless.

Marion hurried to the door and unlocked it. An electronic bell warbled when she pulled it open. "Morning," she said. "You're a few minutes early."

"Rough start to the day," Theo grumbled. "Got coffee and something to eat?"

"Coffee's brewing now." Marion stepped back, inviting the Maple Leafs into the store. "I'm just starting to stock the pastries. Come in."

Sterling moved further behind the wall since he was concerned about being seen. However, it only lasted a moment. What if he had misjudged Marion and she was about to rat out Pearl and Norma Jean? Sterling grabbed a slender rolling pin from a counter. It wasn't like any rolling pin he'd seen before since it didn't have handles. It was just a long, smooth piece of wood. Sterling moved back to the edge of the dividing wall. He peeked around the corner, careful not to expose himself.

The three mobsters filed into the bakery. Rhys entered last and closed the door behind him.

"The storm is really something," Marion said.

"Raining cats and dogs," Rhys said. "Sorry about your floors."

Marion waved her hand. "It's okay. I'll mop up after you leave." She backpedaled toward the kitchen. "Let me bring out some pastries."

Theo clapped his hands. "Can't wait to see what you've got."

Lark said, "You're the only joint open this time of morning."

"Not normally," Marion said over her shoulder as she entered the kitchen. She eyed Sterling and the rolling pin he held. "It'll be fine," she whispered and picked up a large metal tray of pastries.

"What's that?" Rhys asked.

"Just talking to myself." Marion hurried back to the lobby. "Is there something special you're looking for?" She set the tray on the top of the glass counter and the Maple Leafs moved closer to inspect the pastries.

"I'd love a *Chausson aux Pommes*," Theo said. "Got any?"

Sterling had no idea what Theo had just requested.

"They're in the oven now," Marion said. "Should only be another minute or so."

Rhys studied Marion. "You know the cupcake lady?" He snapped his fingers three times. "Norma Jean something or other."

"Oh, sure," Marion said. She moved the pastries from the tray into the glass display rack. "We grew up together."

"Seen her today?"

"How could I do that? I've been here all morning. She's probably down at her shop."

Rhys said, "She's not open."

Marion paused shuffling the pastries. "I'm sorry if that's what you're after. I don't have any cupcakes."

"I'll take a brioche," Lark said, "and a black coffee."

"Same for me," Theo added. "Plus one of those *Chausson aux Pommes* when they're ready."

Marion reached into the display case. "Anything for you?" she asked Rhys.

"A croissant and coffee." The boss looked up from the pastries and toward the kitchen. Sterling ducked out of the way before he could be seen. "What've you got going on back there?"

"What's that?" Marion asked.

"Looks like you might have yourself a leak. Your kitchen floor is wet."

"It's nothing."

"Nothing?"

Marion straightened. "I was cleaning."

"Looks like the floor out here," Rhys said, "except we're wet, and you aren't." The boss's voice turned hard. "How's that happen?"

"I was cleaning," Marion insisted. "Like I said."

"Go and look," Rhys ordered.

"Me?" Theo asked with his mouth full of brioche.

"Both of you."

"Stop," Marion said. "You can't go back there."

Sterling prepared for the Maple Leafs to step into the kitchen. He raised the rolling pin above his head. It didn't matter if Theo or Lark walked through the entryway first, he'd brain either one. Chivalry would get a man killed in a situation like this.

"Maybe I'll take one of those croissants, too," Theo said just as he stepped into the kitchen.

Sterling's rolling pin bounced off Theo's forehead with a loud *thunk*. The strike reverberated along Sterling's arm. It was a sensation Sterling hadn't felt since his days with the Dawgs, and it brought immediate satisfaction.

Theo stiffened and crumpled backward into Lark's arms. "Hey!" she cried as she collapsed underneath the man's weight.

Sterling stepped from behind the wall and made eye contact with Rhys.

"You!" the boss shouted.

Sterling bolted for the back door as fast as his injured ankle would allow him to go, careful not to slip on the wet tiles. The door swung open. For a moment, Sterling thought about hopping off the raised platform to the alley below, but he instinctively knew it was wrong. He hurried down the steps and back into the pouring rain.

Would the Maple Leafs harm Marion Bardot because she helped him? Maybe, Sterling thought. He took a couple of steps toward the east end of the alley and stopped. No, he decided, it was certain they would hurt Marion to get information. Since she knew where Pearl and Norma Jean were hiding, it wouldn't take long for the mobsters to get that information.

Sterling needed to return to the French bakery, but entering through the back door was the wrong choice.

He ran with a hobbling gait toward Main Street, and cut through the small passageway between Chateau Sweets and the neighboring building. When he made the sidewalk, Sterling stopped.

Parked behind the white Lexus was the black BMW, light smoke drifted from its exhaust pipe. Its engine rattled behind the crumpled front-end.

Both Declan and Elliott turned toward him. Sterling prepared to run, but neither thug made a move to get out of their car. Instead, their eyes dropped to the rolling pin Sterling still clutched in his fist. He forgot he had it until that moment.

The wiper blades casually flicked away the rain from BMW's windshield. Declan looked forward and the car slowly pulled away from the curb, its engine clattering in protest. Elliott turned from Sterling as the car headed down Main Street.

Sterling hobbled around the corner and entered Chateau Sweets. The electronic bell warbled and announced his arrival.

Rhys spun. "You!"

Theo still lay on the kitchen floor, but Lark was nowhere to be found. Marion looked panic stricken.

Sterling didn't pause. He stepped forward and Rhys brought his hands up to protect his head. Sterling swung low, cracking the rolling pin across the underboss's thigh. This strike felt as satisfying as the earlier one across Theo's forehead.

Rhys howled in pain and fell to the floor.

Briefly, Sterling lifted the rolling pin in the air, prepared to club the underboss again. Not because the man was a continued threat, but because hitting something felt especially good this morning. It wasn't how a better man would act. He lowered his hand and looked at Marion. "Let's go."

She hurried around the counter. "Maybe you were right."

Rhys rolled left and right, clutching his leg. Sterling didn't believe he broke the man's thigh, but he certainly bruised it. The underboss would walk with a limp for several days.

Sterling grabbed Marion's hand and pulled her after him.

The electronic bell warbled as they exited.

Chapter 14

Sterling paused on the sidewalk, next to the Lexus.

"What are you doing?" Marion asked.

He wanted to disable the car somehow. If the Maple Leafs had to worry about getting this car operational, they'd have less time to focus on finding Pearl. Sterling needed a knife to stab the tires. He needed more time to let the air out of them, a trick he used to play as a rebellious kid.

Sterling could smash the windshield with the rolling pin but that would take time, too. Also, the storm wouldn't hide the sound of him hammering away at the car. He imagined Lark was in the alley. If she heard the noise, she'd come running.

In the end, Sterling decided he couldn't disable the car. He grabbed Marion and hurried across Main Street. Sterling's limped slow them considerably. He pushed Marion in front of him.

"Into the alley," he said.

Marion didn't look back as she hurried through the narrow passageway between two buildings. Sterling sidestepped now, moving considerably slower than Marion due to his size and the width of the corridor.

When he made it to the alley, Sterling stepped out. The rain had flattened Marion's hair, and she looked cold without a coat.

The morning sun was above the horizon now, but the storm clouds still darkened the sky. Marion pointed down the alley. "The bookstore's that way."

When she stepped in the direction of Cozy Corner, Sterling grabbed Marion's arm. "Hold on," he said.

Sterling didn't want to go to the bookstore now. Pearl and Norma Jean were safe. If he and Marion were spotted going into the business, they'd all be at risk.

Lark was certainly searching for them now. Sterling also had to account for Declan and Elliott. Those two abandoned their post a moment before, but that didn't mean they wouldn't have an attack of conscience and come back to the area in hopes of redeeming themselves by doing their duty. The Maple Leafs might even make getting even with Sterling the priority since he assaulted Rhys with the rolling pin.

Sterling couldn't return to his house nor Norma Jean's. Chateau Sweets and Frosty Petal were also eliminated from consideration.

"Take us to your house," Sterling said.

"In this rain? It's ten blocks."

"We can't get any wetter, and we can't go back."

"But the bookstore—"

"We don't want to lead them there."

Marion studied him for a moment. Her wet hair was plastered to her forehead. She untied the apron around her waist and said, "Let's go."

                    ***

Sterling listened for the rattling engine of the
BMW. He worried he might not hear it until too
late because of the storm. They hurried along
Evergreen Street, not slowing to zig or zag.
Sterling considered the strategy but decided
against it.

His limp slowed their journey considerably,
but Sterling suspected Marion didn't mind. She
didn't seem the type for vigorous activity. Her
expression bore the effects of cold and fear.

"It'll be okay," he said, half-heartedly.

Sterling's attitude soured as he considered
the rolling pin he still carried. Fighting with
Theo and Rhys shouldn't have brought him joy,
but Sterling certainly felt something akin to it.
That wasn't how a better man would feel after
striking someone. Was violence so ingrained in
his life that he embraced it at moments like
this? He hoped not.

When he fought with Declan and Elliott,
Sterling didn't feel happy about it. In fact, he
didn't feel anything at all. He just went about
his business.

What was the difference, then?

Maybe the morning had gotten to him. The
rain, the cold, the twisted ankle, and the
possible concussion. Perhaps all those items
created a pressure cooker of frustration.
Smacking the mobsters released some of the
tension. Still, it felt wrong.

Sterling never experienced remorse while he was a member of the Satan's Dawgs. Sure, more than one judge had found him guilty of a crime, but Sterling never felt regret for any actions he committed. He did them for the brotherhood. Even when the club lost its way and Sterling wanted out, he didn't experience guilt. The first time he remembered feeling the emotion was when he turned on the Dawgs and ratted them out to the FBI.

"The rain is slowing," Marion said.

Sterling hadn't noticed since he was lost in thought. Something pierced the sound of the slowing rain now—a rattling engine. He looked over his shoulder but couldn't see its source. Sterling felt confident he knew where it came from.

"How much further?" he asked.

"A couple blocks."

They wouldn't make it in time. "Keep going," he said, "but hurry." Sterling stopped walking and turned around. The pause in movement felt good on his ankle.

"What're you doing?" Marion asked. She stood just behind him.

"The Maple Leafs are almost here. I'll hold them off until you can get home."

"With a rolling pin?"

"Got a gun?" he asked, feeling stupid for earlier throwing away Declan's and Elliott's pistols.

Marion shuffled backward a few steps. "I'll call the police."

He hadn't told her about the flooding and washed-out roads that Marshal Krumland advised, nor had he explained how the cops from Okanogan County were on the way. There wasn't time to do either. "Lock your door," he said over his shoulder.

The rattling engine revved as the crumbled nose of the BMW appeared at the intersection of the next block.

Sterling thought about running but he wanted to give Marion enough time to get to her house. He needed to keep the Maple Leafs occupied so they wouldn't continue looking for Pearl or Norma Jean. He hefted the rolling pin and repeatedly dropped it into his palm. Sterling couldn't shake the feeling that it would feel good to smack Declan and Elliott again.

The BMW's engine accelerated once more, a clattering wind-up that sounded like a raspy smoker's cough. The car turned left and raced toward Sterling. Angry wipers flicked the rain from the windshield.

A few minutes ago, Declan and Elliott had driven casually away from Chateau Sweets. Now it seemed they were itching for a fight. Sterling wondered what changed.

The black sedan skidded to a stop and three car doors opened. Declan and Elliott reluctantly left the driver's and passenger's seats while Lark jumped from the back. She clutched a gun in her hand. Lark was what changed the others' minds.

"Look who it is," she said. "Drop the rolling

pin."

Sterling considered saying something tough like, "Make me," but Lark had a gun. It wasn't a fair fight. Reluctantly, Sterling let go of the pin. It hit the ground and rolled toward the mobsters, eventually stopping when it hit the toe of Elliott's shoe.

"Grab him," Lark said.

"And do what?" Declan asked with his eyes locked onto Sterling.

"We're taking him back to the boss."

"You think he'll tell us where Pearl is?"

Lark laughed once, a cruel chuckle reserved for movie villains and small-town cops. "I think Rhys will want same payback for what he did to Theo and you guys." She waggled the gun between Sterling and the other mobsters. "Get moving."

Declan and Elliott exchanged glances. It was clear by the expressions on their faces that they didn't want to approach Sterling.

"What're you waiting for?" Lark asked, her face pinched with anger.

"It's okay," Sterling said. "Give them a minute."

Lark leveled the gun at his head. "You stay out of this."

Declan jerked his head toward Sterling. "We've got no choice," he said.

Elliott's shoulders slumped. "When do we ever?"

"Now," Lark demanded.

"All right," Declan said. "We're going." His

eyes narrowed as he studied Sterling. "I'm warning you—no funny stuff."

Elliott nodded. "Yeah. No surprises this time."

Sterling raised his hands in surrender. He had no intention of fighting now, not while Lark pointed her gun at him. She seemed willing to shoot him for a perceived slight.

Declan moved between Lark and Sterling, his hands up and ready for any attack.

Elliott warily stepped over the rolling pin. His eyes were locked onto Sterling's. "Try anything and I'll—"

Sterling lowered his hands slightly and Elliott jerked back, clearly afraid Sterling was making some sort of move. His heel dropped onto the rolling pin, and he lost his balance. Elliott tumbled backward into the BMW, falling as he went. He cracked his skull on the crumbled bumper, then slumped sideways onto the wet asphalt.

Declan, apparently afraid Sterling was indeed attacking, jumped back into Lark and her gun fired. He howled in pain and grabbed his shoulder, twirling in the street like a wayward top.

For his part, Sterling remained standing with his hands in the air, albeit slightly lower now.

"You shot me!" Declan cried.

Lark pointed her gun at Sterling. "It was your fault."

"You *shot* me!"

"Stop it," she said. "I shot you in the shoulder. You're not going to die."

Declan examined the blood on his hand. "I need a doctor."

"When we get home."

"I need help now!"

"We'll get you some bandages." Lark tapped Elliott's foot with her own. "Get up."

The fallen man didn't stir.

Declan's face twisted with anger, and he kicked in Sterling's direction. "You did this. It's your fault."

"Me?" Sterling raised his hands a bit higher. It seemed an appropriate time to display his willingness to surrender.

Lark tsked. "Stop being a baby, Declan. He scared you. Admit it."

"You didn't see him." Declan kicked at Sterling again. "He lunged."

She eyed Sterling. "Didn't look like he lunged."

"He did," Declan said. "He most definitely did."

"He's not lunging now." Lark tapped the fallen man's foot again. "Check on Elliott. See if he's dead."

"He better not be." Declan leaned over and shook Elliott. "Get up." The unconscious man didn't move. Declan straightened. "He's breathing."

"Pick him up," Lark said to Sterling, "and put him in the car."

Sterling's eyes cut to the unconscious man. The rolling pin lay underneath Elliott's calf. His gaze returned to Lark. "I've gotta lower my hands."

"Don't be a moron." She waggled the gun. "Get a move on, and if you touch the roller, I'll shoot you where you stand."

"Just do it now," Declan pleaded.

"No. The boss'll have some questions."

"C'mon, Lark. We'll tell Rhys this guy didn't give you any choice. He was begging to be shot."

Sterling's hands remained in the air. "Nobody has to shoot me."

"Shut up, you," Declan snapped.

"I'm not shooting him," Lark said, "and that's final." Her eyes narrowed. "Unless he touches the rolling pin, then all bets are off."

"I'm not going anywhere near the roller," Sterling said. He lowered his hands and slipped his arms around Elliott.

"He's going for the pin!" Declan hollered and pointed. "Shoot him!"

Sterling froze with his arms around Elliott's torso. His gaze drifted toward Lark.

"Ignore him," she said.

Declan sighed. "You watch. You're going to regret not shooting him when you had the chance."

Sterling stood. He shuffled left and right as he struggled to get Elliott off the ground. Stabilizing himself with a bad ankle while picking up an unconscious man was no easy feat. Lifting a 200-pound bag of potatoes would've been easier since it didn't have arms and legs flopping and swinging as it moved. Elliott's head lulled to the side and bounced off

Sterling's shoulder. He made sure not to step on the rolling pin. "Where do you want him?"

"Back seat, behind the passenger." Lark looked at Declan and jerked her head toward the car. "Open the door."

"Why don't you? I'm the one shot."

"I'm the one smart enough not to lose my gun," she said. "Go."

Declan grunted his displeasure, but he opened the rear car door and stepped out of the way for Sterling.

Stuffing an unconscious man into the rear seat of a car was a bit like shoving toothpaste back into a tube. It wasn't impossible but doing it alone certainly wasn't easy. Sterling dropped Elliott onto the seat.

"Easy with him," Declan said.

Sterling sat Elliott upright and pushed his legs into the car. The unconscious man fell over. Sterling shut the door.

"Get behind the wheel," Lark said.

Sterling nodded. "Whatever you say."

Declan winced as he grabbed his shoulder. "I'm begging you. Put him out of our misery."

"Stop whining," Lark said. "You sit in the passenger seat."

She kept her gun pointed at Sterling until he climbed into the car, then she sat behind him. There was no way for him to turn around and take the gun from her. Declan settled into the passenger seat.

Sterling pressed the Start button and the engine rattled to life. "Where to?"

"Don't get cute," Lark said. "You know exactly where we're going."

***

Sterling turned onto Main Street and pulled the BMW to the curb in front of Chateau Sweets. He parked behind the Lexus and turned the engine off.

"Get out," Lark said.

Declan sneered at Sterling. "You're in for it now."

Sterling stepped out of the car. He briefly thought about running, but he wouldn't get far on his bad ankle before Lark shot him in the back. As soon as he left the driver's seat, Lark was out of the car with the gun clutched in her fist.

"Let's go," she said.

"Want me to grab your friend?" Sterling motioned toward the still unconscious Elliott.

"Leave him and walk."

The sign on the bakery's door read *Closed*, and the door was locked. Lark tapped on the glass with the barrel of her gun.

In a moment, Theo opened the door. A bump the size of a goose egg had grown on his forehead. "Where you been? The boss has been calling."

"I left my phone in the car," Lark said. "We brought Rhys a present." She motioned toward Sterling.

Theo leaned out of the store to get a better

view. His eyes widened when he saw Sterling. "You!" He stepped onto the sidewalk. "I'm gonna kill you so fast—"

"No you're not," Lark said. She held up her arm to stop Theo. "Not till the boss gets to talk with him." She looked into the bakery. "Where is he?"

"Sitting in the back. Might have a broken leg because of this guy."

"What happened to your head?" Declan asked.

Theo flicked his hand at Sterling. "What do you think?"

Lark lifted her chin. "Handsome here smacked Theo with a rolling pin."

"Where's Elliott?" Theo asked, gingerly touching the massive bump on his head.

"He's in the car, unconscious," Lark said. "Knocked himself out."

"How?"

"You wouldn't believe me if I told you."

Declan grunted. "Can we get out of the rain so I can get some help?"

Theo nodded but didn't move. He just leaned further out of the door to study Declan. "What happened to you?"

"The big guy lunged," Declan said, jerking his head at Sterling. "Then she shot me."

Lark rolled her eyes. "That's not how it went down."

Theo said, "I bet the big fella had a hand in taking out Elliott, too."

Declan nodded. "You know it."

Sterling's gaze drifted up and down Main Street. Where was all the traffic? Marshal Krumland mentioned flooding to the south. Was it diverting traffic away from Wandering Springs? Still, the locals would be out soon or was the morning shower keeping them all inside? Sterling found the last question hard to believe since this area was known for its rain.

The bigger question became how long the Maple Leafs would stay in town before they decided it was too risky. Had Sterling's actions caused them to stay longer so they could get even with him? If Norma Jean and Pearl were safe, he supposed it was okay.

"Hey," Lark said, breaking into Sterling's private thoughts. "Inside."

Theo shuffled backward and Sterling stepped through the door. Someone pushed Sterling's shoulder, and he stumbled inside, his bad ankle wasn't prepared for the sudden lurch. The three Maple Leafs hurried inside the bakery and Theo locked the door behind them.

"Come on," Lark said with a waggle of her gun. "You got a date with the boss."

Sterling limped around the glass display case and into the kitchen. Rhys sat on a desk chair he must've pulled out of the nearby office. He held a gun in both hands. It was the one he'd taken from Theo.

"Well, well," Rhys said. He rose out of the chair but scowled when he put weight on his leg. "If it isn't the rock in my shoe."

"How's the leg?" Lark asked with obvious

concern in her voice.

The boss shifted his gaze to her. "He hit me with a roller. How do you think it feels?"

"Probably as good as my shoulder," Declan said.

"And my head," Theo added.

"Where's Elliott?"

"In the car," Theo said. "Big boy knocked him out."

Rhys sneered. "That so?"

"It was an accident," Lark said evenly. "Elliott did it to himself."

The other Maple Leafs turned to her, various stages of surprise in their eyes.

"Why do you keep defending him?" Declan asked.

"I'm not," Lark said.

Theo pointed at her. "She is. Totally."

Rhys nodded slowly. "Chivalry paid off, eh? The big guy didn't smack you because you're a lady, so you feel like you owe him one. That it?"

"I don't owe him anything," Lark said. She pointed the gun at Sterling. "Give the word and I'll put a hole in him."

"There will be time for that." Rhys tucked his gun into his coat pocket. He winced as he settled into the chair. When he overcame the pain, he studied Sterling. "You look surprisingly good for a man who's laid waste to my entire crew."

"Not entire," Declan said.

Theo scoffed as his eyes cut to Lark. "Yeah, not entire."

Sterling didn't think it would help his situation to explain he had a sprained ankle and that he might have a concussion.

"All this because you work for some cupcake lady?" Rhys scrunched his nose. "I'm not buying it. Nobody plays the good Samaritan anymore."

"You were going to hurt Norma Jean," Sterling said.

"We didn't care about her."

"Pearl, then. You were going to hurt her."

Rhys spread his arms wide. "What can I say? Guilty as charged." It looked as if he wanted to smile but the boss cringed in pain. "Where is she?"

"I won't tell you."

"Yeah," Rhys said, "I believe you won't. You didn't stick around and cause all this mayhem just to rat her out."

Theo stepped forward. "We're not giving up, are we?"

"We've got no choice." Rhys stood and grunted. The pain he felt in his leg was obvious. "We've made too much noise. I'm surprised the cops aren't already here. We need to get moving and get back across the border."

"I need a doctor," Declan said, "for my shoulder."

The boss frowned. "We all need a doctor."

"Not all of us," Theo said, his eyes once again cutting to Lark.

"Don't blame me for keeping my gun, idiot," she said. Lark pointed it at Theo for emphasis.

Sterling wasn't prepared to take advantage of

her looking away from him. His attention had wandered as he watched the interaction between the other Maple Leafs.

"Enough," Rhys said, waving a hand to interrupt the quarreling. "Shoot this guy and let's be on our way."

Lark raised her gun while Declan and Theo scrambled back so as not to get hit by an errant bullet or perhaps to avoid blood spatter.

"Hold on!" Sterling said, leaning away from the gun and bringing up his hand for protection. "Hold on."

"What now?" Rhys said. "Suddenly got a change of heart?"

Sterling had one card to play. "I'm worth more to you alive than dead."

Rhys chuckled. "We don't need a hostage. We got friends on the border." He flicked his hand. "Shoot him."

"Wait!" Sterling said. He lifted both hands in front of his face. The act wouldn't stop a bullet, but it felt natural. The same way a man falling from an airplane might convince himself he could fly if he flapped his arms hard enough. "I'm not talking as a hostage."

Rhys eyed Lark. "Hold off, but the next time I tell you to shoot him, do it without hesitation."

"Happy to," she said, pointing the gun at Sterling's head.

The boss crossed his arms. "You got one chance to save your life, eh? Better make it good."

Sterling lowered his hands. Either the Maple

Leafs would buy what he was about to say, or Lark would shoot him immediately. No matter which happened, his life would be radically different in the next minute.

"My name isn't Sterling Carter," he said.

Rhys furrowed his brow. "What are you talking about? We got your wallet. We know what your driver's license says."

"He's stalling," Theo said. "Shoot him."

Declan nodded. "Yeah. Let's be on our way. I need a doctor."

Lark eyed Rhys expectantly, but he shook his head.

Sterling tried his best to look contrite. "You caught me. I give up."

The assembled Maple Leafs shared confused glances.

"I'm in the Witness Protection Program," Sterling said.

Theo and Declan laughed, and Lark smirked behind her raised gun.

"You're what now?" Rhys asked.

"The Witness Protection Program," Sterling said.

The boss angrily waved his hand. "Don't give me that."

"It's the truth."

"The same program as Pearl?"

"The American program."

Rhys furrowed his brow. "Let's say I believe you."

"You don't," Theo blurted. "Do you?"

"Hold on," the boss said. "Let's hear him out.

Tell us, tough guy, why are you in the program?"

"That's a long story."

"One you don't have time for," Rhys said. "Make it snappy."

"I provided information to the U.S. government."

Theo raised his fist. "He's a snitch!"

"A stoolie," Declan added. "Just like Pearl. Why are you even thinking about this, boss? Let's waste him and get me to a doctor."

"I'll agree he's not our problem," Rhys said, "but maybe we've got some counterparts who'd owe us a favor if we delivered him." He eyed Lark. "Lower it."

She reluctantly dropped her hand and stepped further away from Sterling. She'd have plenty of time to raise it again if he tried anything.

"Okay, fella," Rhys said, "time for the truth. What's your real name?"

Chapter 15

"Beauregard Smith," Rhys said into his cell phone. "Uh-huh. That's right. The American program. I know we don't have access to their database, maybe you can call someone and check."

Sterling stood in the bakery's kitchen with his arms crossed. He glanced at the various utensils within his reach—a whisk, spatula, and heavy wooden spoon.

Lark leveled the barrel of the gun. "Stop looking around. You're making me nervous."

"Can't believe we're wasting time for a rat," Theo muttered.

Rhys held his hand over his open ear and moved further away from the group.

"What do you want us to do?" Lark asked Theo.

He thumbed at Sterling. "We dump this guy and hit the road. We can worry about Pearl later."

"What if he proves to be somebody worth grabbing?"

Theo scoffed. "He's a baker."

"Assistant baker," Sterling clarified.

"See?" Theo asked. "Nobody wants this guy."

"If he's in the program," Lark said, "don't you want to know what he did on the outside?"

Declan tsked, then said, "I'll be back."

"Where you going?" Lark asked.

"To check on Elliott." He headed for the lobby.

She jerked her head toward the front of the store. "Lock the door behind him."

"Why me?" Theo asked.

"Because I've got the gun."

"Blah blah blah. Whatever."

The electronic bell warbled as Declan went outside.

Rhys covered the phone's receiver. "They're making some calls now."

"Could we do this on the road?" Lark asked.

"Better to do it now," the boss said. "If he's somebody, we take him with us."

"If he's not?"

The boss's gaze slid to Sterling. "There's no good outcome for you, you know that."

Sterling shrugged. He knew that, of course, but the longer the Maple Leafs took investigating his background, the less time they spent worried about Pearl and Norma Jean.

"Hey boss," Theo called from the front of the bakery, "we got a problem."

Rhys lifted his elbow toward Theo. "Find out what he's talking about."

Lark motioned toward her gun, then Sterling. "Want me to leave him alone with you?"

"On second thought." The boss's face darkened. "Call Theo back here."

"Theo!" she shouted over her shoulder.

Rhys cringed. "Quietly," he said. "I'm still on the phone."

Theo soon appeared. "There's people out

front.”

“People?” Rhys asked.

“Customers.”

“Get rid of them.”

Theo nodded and hurried away.

Rhys eyed Lark. “I think that bump on his head is making him dumber.”

“You’re giving him too much credit,” she said.

The electronic bell warbled again and Theo said something Sterling couldn’t make out. Then there was murmuring from others. Perhaps Sterling should yell for help, but that would get someone else involved in this morning’s turmoil.

“Whatever you’re thinking,” Lark said, “knock it off.”

Sterling raised his hands. “I could tell you how to look it up on the internet.”

“How’s that?”

“They’ve got a website.”

Her brow furrowed. “Who?”

“The mob.”

“The mob?”

“Thefbiisabunchofdirtyrats.com tracks everyone they suspect is in the witness program.”

Lark smirked. “They copied that from us. We did it first. Themountiesareabandofrottenfinks.com. Lets everyone know who is in the program.”

Sterling frowned. If it was true the Maple Leafs created their tracking database first, then it was one more reason Sterling had to question his opinion of Canada. Was their criminal element better equipped than their counterparts to the south? Sterling hated to believe that after all the trouble various factions of the American mob had given him recently. Yet, it was the Maple Leafs who now held him.

"Uh-huh," Rhys said into the phone, "still here. No, no, I'd rather wait. Get it right the first time."

Theo returned to the kitchen with Declan and Elliott in tow. Declan still held his shoulder and Elliott pressed a hand to the back of his head.

"What're we doing?" Elliott mumbled. He looked woozy and his voice sounded weak.

"This guy's a stoolie," Declan said, lifting his chin toward Sterling.

"An American snitch," Theo clarified.

Declan continued. "The boss is on the phone with the higher ups to see what they want us to do."

Elliott frowned. "I say we shoot the squealer and get out of this town. It's been nothing but bad luck since we got here."

"Nobody's shooting nobody," Rhys said. "Not until I say so."

"Lark shot me," Declan said.

"Shut your trap," Rhys said. To the phone, he clarified, "Not you. Sorry. What were you saying? Uh-huh. Right." His upper lip curled as his eyes settled on Sterling. "An enforcer? For real?"

"I knew it," Theo said. He snapped his fingers and pointed at Sterling. "The guy's an enforcer."

"No wonder he got the drop on us," Declan said. "A wolf in sheep's clothing."

Lark stepped further back, and she raised the gun with both hands.

"Okay, yeah," Rhys said. "We understand. We're on it." He hung up the phone. "Well, well, well. Looks like we bagged ourselves an elephant."

Elliott leaned against the wall. He appeared about to throw up. "How's that?"

"Ol' Beauregard Smith here is wanted by some motorcycle club in Arizona."

"What do we care about that?" Declan asked.

"He's also wanted by our brothers down south."

"The Mexicans?" Theo asked.

Rhys cocked his head. "The Americans. How hard did he hit you?"

Theo gently touched the bump on his forehead. "He got me good."

"What's the plan?" Lark asked.

"We're taking him with us," Rhys said.

"And Pearl?"

"We don't have time to find her." Rhys hobbled toward the back door. "We take this one with us when we leave. We'll worry about Pearl another time."

"But we've got her on the run," Lark objected. "Think how much time it took to find her."

"Yeah," Theo said. "I vote we shoot this guy and keep searching for Pearl."

"I need a doctor," Declan whined.

"This isn't our choice anymore," Rhys said.

"We take the tough guy with us, and deliver him to the Americans when we're safe."

Sterling frowned. "You could have them pick me up here. Save us both a couple of border crossings."

"Shut up, you," Rhys said. To the others, he said, "We've got orders, and we're going to follow them."

"How are we going to get him across the border?" Declan asked.

"Don't you worry about that. The bosses said they'd grease the skids. All we got to do is get there."

Someone banged on the front door. Theo moved to look around the corner. "More customers," he said.

"Our cars are out front," Declan said.

Rhys rolled his eyes. "I know that. One of you, bring my car around back."

Declan, Elliott, and Theo looked at Lark.

"He meant one of you," she said. "I'm still the one with a gun."

"Don't any of you think I forgot about that either," Rhys said. "We're gonna deal with you losing your guns once we're home."

Theo's eyes widened. "You took my gun. I didn't lose it."

"After you shot the car," Lark said. "Twice."

"How were we to know the guy was an enforcer?" Declan asked.

Rhys's eyes narrowed. "You're all enforcers, too. Or did you forget?"

Declan clucked. "Still."

"Go," the boss said, "both of you." He waggled his hand at Declan and Theo. "Get the cars and bring them around. I'll lock the door behind you."

The two men wandered off toward the lobby. Rhys followed with an extreme limp. The electronic bell signaled their exit.

Lark held the gun steady with both hands. She stood in a classic police stance—legs wide and arms held at a V. She wasn't going to be surprised by Sterling.

Rhys returned to the kitchen, grimacing with each step. As he passed the still leaning Elliott he paused to study him. The other man's eyes were closed, and he held his stomach. Lark's eyes slid to them.

Sterling thought there might not be a better time to make something happen. The Maple Leafs were once again divided. He had no idea how they expected to transport him. If he was in a trunk again, his chances of escape diminished greatly. If they put him in the back seat with Lark, he doubted she'd make any of the mistakes the other mobsters had made.

He had to move and it had to be now. He took a small sidestep toward the counter where the variety of baking tools lay.

Lark turned to him. "What're you doing?"

"Just standing here," he said.

"You don't look so good," Rhys said to Elliott.

"I don't feel so hot either." Elliott groaned. "Feels like church bells ringing inside my head."

Lark's gaze drifted to the man leaning against

the wall. "You fell pretty hard."

Without looking, Sterling reached for the heavy wooden spoon on the nearby counter. Grabbing a utensil, he recrossed his arms, hiding the implement. The round steel handle in his hand felt cool. Even without looking, Sterling knew which utensil he'd grabbed. Unfortunately, it wasn't the one he wanted.

Elliott lifted his head and his gaze settled on Sterling. "I fell because he hit me."

"You tripped," Lark said.

"On what?"

"The rolling pin."

Elliott's eyes narrowed. "He planned it."

An engine rattled out on Main Street, much louder than the continued knocking on the front door. In a moment, the BMW would drive away, turn the corner, and enter the alley. When it and the Lexus pulled behind Chateau Sweets, Sterling's window for escape was likely gone. He needed to act now.

"Get ready," Rhys said. "They're coming into the alley."

The boss hobbled to the back door, flinching with each step.

Elliott pointed at Sterling. "I owe you one."

"There will be time for that later," Lark said.

"Easy for you to say, he didn't hit you."

Lark rolled her eyes. "He didn't hit you, either."

"Knock it off you two," Rhys said. "Let's go."

Hoping to rile up Elliott, Sterling said, "I hit him."

"See?" Elliott said.

"That was before you slipped on the roller." Sterling bobbled his head. "If we want to get technical, I hit you twice."

"That's it." Elliott stepped woozily forward, moving between Sterling and Lark. He hunched and brought his fists up.

Sterling uncrossed his arms now, exposing the whisk he clutched in his left hand.

Elliott paused and blurted, "What the—?"

"Get out of the way," Lark said. "You're blocking my shot."

Rhys flicked his hand. "It's a beater. What's he gonna do with that?"

Sterling slapped Elliott across the face before the man could get within punching range, then swiped it in the opposite direction like a tennis player smashing a backhand shot.

Elliott stiffened, more surprised than hurt. He lowered his hands. "That's not right."

"Move," Lark ordered, but Elliott didn't listen.

He took an unsure half-step forward when Sterling slapped him twice more with the whisk. Red stripes blossomed on the thug's cheeks.

"Elliott!" Rhys barked.

"What?" Elliott shouted and turned to look at his boss.

Sterling stepped forward and punched the man across the chin. Elliott crumpled to the floor.

Lark brought up her gun. "Give the word, boss."

"We have our orders," Rhys said. "He's

coming with us."

"What if he tries something stupid again?"

"Shoot him in the leg. There were no orders against him being damaged."

Lark smiled. "You hear that?"

Sterling had. He dropped the whisk and lifted his hands in the air.

A rattling engine pulled up behind the bakery. In a moment, the back door opened, and Theo stuck his head in. When he saw Elliott lying on the floor, he asked, "What happened?"

Rhys thumbed toward Sterling. "Tough guy hit Elliott with a whisk."

"Must've been some whisk," Theo said.

***

The rain continued to pour as four of them stood outside. Elliott remained on the bakery floor. The trunk of the Lexus was open.

Rhys said, "Get in."

Lark's gun remained trained on Sterling. "You heard the man."

Sterling quickly considered the odds. Rhys had a bum leg, Theo's forehead carried a goose egg, and Declan clutched his shoulder where he'd been shot. Under normal circumstances, Sterling liked those odds. While most of the effects from his possible concussion seemed to have dissipated, Sterling's ankle remained sprained. Above all, Lark and her gun remained out of reach.

Reluctantly, he climbed into the trunk.

Theo moved closer. "This is for Elliott." He punched down, but Sterling brought his arms up to protect his head. Theo's fist crunched against Sterling's elbow and the man howled in pain. "My hand!" He spun away from the trunk.

"Boss," Declan said. His attention was down the alley. "Look."

Rhys turned. "The cops," he muttered. He motioned toward the trunk. "Shut it."

Lark stepped forward and slammed the lid closed.

Outside, there were hurried, muffled voices. Suddenly, the car lurched forward and hit a pothole. Sterling bounced in the darkness of the trunk.

He couldn't judge the car's speed, but it felt fast. He was jostled a couple more times, each less violent than the previous, until the car's back end slid as it turned right. The car abruptly stopped, its tires squealing on the wet ground. Sterling was tossed around some more.

Voices surrounded the vehicle now, shouting orders such as "Get out of the car!" and "Show us your hands!"

Sterling pounded his fist on the underside of the trunk lid. He didn't shout, though. With all the yelling and the pouring rain, he didn't think his voice would make much difference. He wasn't even sure if hitting the trunk would get anyone's attention, yet he kept it up.

When the trunk finally opened, light flooded in. An Okanogan County Sheriff's deputy stood over Sterling. "It's over," the officer said. "You can get out now."

Chapter 16

A crowd gathered around the front of Chateau Sweets. They clutched umbrellas as they watched the activity inside the bakery with interest.

Deputy Joe Armstrong sipped coffee before setting the cup on top of the glass display case. He wore a brown raincoat over his brown and tan uniform. When he finished writing in his notebook, the deputy looked up. "That's when the woman shot her partner in the shoulder?"

"That's right," Sterling said.

Armstrong nodded. "I think I'm following. What happened next?"

Before Sterling could answer, another deputy knocked on the front door. Armstrong said, "Hold on," and walked over to unlock it.

Norma Jean and Pearl came in with the other lawman. When the women saw Sterling, their eyes widened.

"Silver!" Norma Jean exclaimed. She hurried over and hugged him.

Sterling wasn't much of a hugger, but he returned the gesture. Norma Jean held him like his grandmother used to do.

"She was worried about you," Pearl said.

"We both were," Norma Jean said as she broke their embrace. "Don't let her fool you." She glanced around. "Where's Marion?"

"Her house," Sterling said. "We came up with a Plan B. A deputy is on his way to get her now."

"What about the Maple Leafs?" Pearl asked.

"They're in handcuffs. Cooling off in the back of a couple patrol cars."

"Excuse me," Deputy Armstrong said, "we need to get back to our interview. I'll be with you ladies in a moment."

Norma Jean nodded. "Totally understand."

Pearl gestured toward the kitchen. "You think Marion would mind if I had another croissant?"

Sterling stepped away from the others with Deputy Armstrong.

"Where were we?" the lawman asked.

"You asked what happened after the woman shot her partner?"

Armstrong opened his notepad. "Right. Let's pick it up from there."

Sterling told the deputy everything about the incident. There was no need to hold anything back about the Maple Leafs or why they were after Norma Jean and Pearl. When he finished relaying the details, Sterling fell silent and watched the deputy write in his notebook.

Armstrong looked up. "You're very calm for someone who just went through this situation."

"I'll freak out later."

The deputy smiled. "Of course. Don't leave yet. I might have a follow-up question or two."

Armstrong walked over to Pearl and Norma Jean. Pearl happily ate a croissant and sipped coffee. The deputy said something to the two women, then Norma Jean headed toward

Sterling.

"What a morning," she said. "Ever been involved with something like this?"

He had several times since he'd arrived in Witness Protection, but Sterling kept that to himself.

Norma Jean continued. "I gotta say, Silver. You sure came through for Pearl. I can't tell you how much I appreciate it."

"Anyone would have done it."

"Don't sell yourself short. Not many would put their lives on the line for someone they didn't know."

Sterling wasn't sure of that. He wanted to be a better man than he was while with the Dawgs. It wouldn't take much to be an improved version of himself. However, he imagined most men—those with pride and dignity—would have come to Pearl's aid. Sterling believed most women would have as well. Good people came to the aid of others.

"You helped her," Sterling said.

Norma Jean waved off his comment. "She's my friend. My best customer, too." Her eyes cut to Pearl. "Although she's getting awfully friendly with those croissants."

The electronic bell warbled at the front door and Marion Bardot entered. Her gaze bounced around the lobby. She was accompanied by another deputy who motioned for her to stand off to the side. Marion didn't go where he pointed, however. Instead, she headed for Sterling and Norma Jean.

"Did they catch them all?" she asked.

"They did," Sterling said.

"Why's everyone in my store?"

"It was the last place we were before the cops showed up."

Marion frowned as she looked through the customers outside the window. Many of them were starting to walk away. "Look at all the sales I'm losing this morning"

"Cheer up," Norma Jean said. "At least we're both closed."

"Not exactly sure that can be considered a bright side." Marion turned her attention to Sterling. "You're okay?"

"It wasn't anything that hasn't happened before," he said.

The two women seemed confused by his statement.

Sterling pointed at his foot. "Twisted ankle, I mean." He left out his possible concussion. The fogginess in his head had mostly dissipated.

"What happens now?" Norma Jean asked.

"The deputies finish their interviews," Sterling said, "and we go about our lives."

"And Pearl?"

"I suppose the Mounties will come and get her. She'll move to a new city and get a new name."

Norma Jean looked at her friend who happily noshed on a pastry. "This is the last time I'm going to see her?"

"Probably," Sterling said.

She sighed. "I guess that's how life goes. An

old friend leaves our lives, and a new one enters.”

Marion put her hand on Norma Jean’s shoulder. “Or an old friend re-enters.”

Norma Jean smiled. “I suppose so.”

“Would you two like something from the kitchen?” Marion asked. “I want to go see if any damage was done back there.”

“Nothing for me,” Sterling said.

“Since you’re asking,” Norma Jean said, “I guess I should have one of those croissants to see what Pearl is so excited about.”

Marion hurried into the kitchen.

“Well, Silver, tomorrow is going to feel different around here.”

Sterling didn’t respond. He knew what was going to happen once the marshals made their way to Wandering Springs. He’d be whisked away just like Pearl.

“What’d we learn today?” she asked.

Sterling thought back on the morning until he landed on something. “I learned what a moggy was.”

Norma Jean raised an eyebrow. “How could you not know about moggies?”

***

Travis watched as Sterling shoved several pairs of socks into his bag.

“It won’t be so bad,” he said to the cat. “We’ve got some time to get ready.”

Sterling paused, hoping to read some

recognition on the tom's face. Not getting any, he continued thrusting clothes into the bag. "I think Krumland's finally on our side. No way he can say this is my fault now."

Travis flopped to the ground and stretched out, his front paws reaching for his kicker fish toy.

"It'll do us good to get away from the border," Sterling said. "Too many Canadians isn't good for anyone."

The cat snatched the toy, flipped it to its belly, and kicked it repeatedly with its back feet.

Sterling grabbed the latest paperback he purchased—*Burglars Can't be Choosers*—and slipped it into the bag.

Preparing for relocation was simple. Sterling didn't need to bring furniture or food. He didn't have any knickknacks or memorabilia hung around his neck like an albatross.

Sterling remembered the albatross symbolism from *The Rime of the Ancient Mariner*, not because his high school English teacher insisted his class read the poem, but rather because Iron Maiden recorded a nearly fourteen-minute song retelling the story to blazing guitars, pounding drums, and piercing vocals. Sterling thought most high school lessons should've been taught that way.

Someone knocked on the front door.

"That's our ride," Sterling said.

He zipped up his bag but left it sitting on his bed. He didn't collect Travis yet. Sterling would do that in a moment.

When he opened the door, a small black man with wire-rimmed glasses smiled up at him. He wore a tailored suit with shined shoes. Behind him, parked at the curb, was a black Chevy Suburban.

"Beauregard Smith?" the man asked.

"That depends."

"Of course." He pulled his suit jacket to the side to reveal a star within a circular ring attached to his belt. It was the U.S. Marshals badge and it sat next to a holstered pistol. "Marshal Ezra Heffley. I've been assigned to get you to safety."

"You're alone?"

"For this leg of your journey."

"Where are we going?"

Heffley shrugged. "Don't know yet. Right now, we need to get on the road and put some distance between you and Wandering Springs. Word is some unfriendly forces are already headed this way."

Forces, Sterling thought. The marshal was likely talking about the Satan's Dawgs or a faction of the U.S. mob. Perhaps the Maple Leafs were now after him, too. Since joining the program, more people than ever wanted to kill him.

"Is Krumland on his way?"

Heffley shook his head. "Lester's out. I'm the relief pitcher."

"You're my new witness inspector?"

"That's right. I drew the short straw." Heffley didn't smile. "Are you packed?"

Sterling thumbed over his shoulder. "My bag's ready. I just have to grab my cat."

The marshal's expression darkened. "Leave it."

"The cat?"

"I'm allergic." As if on cue, the marshal sneezed.

"I'm not leaving the cat."

"He can't ride with us," Heffley said as he scratched the back of his hand. "I'll break out in hives."

"Oh, no," Sterling said flatly. "Hives."

Heffley's eyes narrowed. "Your sympathy is noted."

"I'm not leaving my moggy."

"Moggy?"

"How do you not know what a moggy is?"

Heffley's upper lip curled. "You wanna walk?"

"I don't even know where I'm going."

"Exactly."

"Whatever, man," Sterling said. "We'll find our own way." He started to close the door, but the marshal put his hand out, stopping it from closing.

"Hold on." Heffley glanced over his shoulder at his SUV, then turned his attention back to Sterling. "Bring the cat, but we ride with the windows down."

"Whatever you say." Sterling cocked his head. "But I don't think Travis will like it."

Beau Smith
returns in...

Cozy Up
to Chaos

Did You Enjoy the Book?

Thank you for reading *Cozy Up to Mayhem*! This is a continuing series with Beau visiting new locations under other assumed identities. I hope you'll check the other books out.

I'm always grateful when a reader takes time out of their day to comment on one of my novels. If you do write a review, please email me, and let me know.

I'd love to say thanks!

-   Colin

About the Author

Besides writing the Cozy Up Series, Colin Conway is the author of the 509 Crime Stories, a series of novels set in Eastern Washington with revolving lead characters. They are standalone tales and can be read in any order.

Colin is also the co-author of the Charlie-316 series. The first book in the series, Charlie-316, is a political/crime thriller and has been described as "riveting and compulsively readable," "the real deal," and "the ultimate ride-along."

He served in the U.S. Army and later was an officer of the Spokane Police Department. He has owned a laundromat, invested in a bar, and run a karate school. Besides writing crime fiction, he is a commercial real estate broker.

Colin lives with his beautiful girlfriend, three wonderful children, and a codependent Vizsla that rules their world.

Learn more at colinconway.com